THE
FLOATING
CIRCUS

ALSO BY TRACIE VAUGHN ZIMMER

Reaching for Sun

THE
FLOATING
CIRCUS

TRACIE VAUGHN ZIMMER

BLOOMSBURY
CHILDREN'S
BOOKS

Published by Bloomsbury U.S.A. Children's Books
175 Fifth Avenue, New York, New York 10010
Distributed to the trade by Macmillan

Library of Congress Cataloging-in-Publication Data
Zimmer, Tracie Vaughn.
The floating circus / by Tracie Vaughn Zimmer. — 1st U.S. ed.
p.   cm.
Summary: In 1850s Pittsburgh, thirteen-year-old Owen leaves his younger brother
and sneaks aboard a circus housed in a riverboat, where he befriends a freed slave,
learns to work with elephants, and finally comes to terms with the choices he has
made in his difficult life.
ISBN-13: 978-1-59990-185-5 • ISBN-10: 1-59990-185-4 (hardcover)
[1. Abandoned children—Fiction.   2. Circus—Fiction.   3. River boats—Fiction.]
I. Title.
PZ7.Z6165F12008   [Fic]—dc22   2007038998

First U.S. Edition 2008
Typeset by Westchester Book Composition
Printed in the U.S.A. by Quebecor World Fairfield
1 3 5 7 9 10 8 6 4 2

THE
FLOATING
CIRCUS

CHAPTER

1

I SHOULDA LISTENED to my brother. Right follows Zach like a shadow, but wrong wears me like a skin. That rotten-mouthed Simeon wagered me his bread for a week if I could touch the roof of the orphanage. The nag in my stomach could get me to do most anything, and the roof didn't seem but a stretch higher than my usual spot. Every afternoon I'd scramble up there to try to catch a glimpse of Momma on the busy streets of Pittsburgh. Skinny enough to see through, I was sure I could make it to the top of that tree fast as a squirrel. And I nearly did, too. When the branches started to bend and crackle under my weight, did it stop me? Heck, no. I wrapped my fingers around the branches and kept pulling myself toward sky.

My brother, Zach, called up to me, "Get back down here, Owen! I'll throw sticks like you want."

"No! I'm bored sick of that game!"

At first, all the kids at the orphanage, even the ones who just learned how to walk, watched me start up the tree. Shading their eyes from the spring sun, they followed me. But it's a mighty big tree and little ones— why, they lose interest fast. When I looked back down again, they'd scattered like chickens, plucking in the dirt or chasing each other around. I liked it better with an audience. Always had. I knew if I got close to the roof they'd all come back to see, and they did.

I called to them: "Boys and girls! Lice magnets! Wastrels! Do not miss this daring exhibition of human skill. Owen Burke is a one-of-a-kind. Why, even monkeys in the jungles try to imitate his ways! He's an American marvel." Now all the kids were staring again. The little ones waved at me, and I waved back and smiled.

Though it made me teeter a bit, I cupped my hands around my mouth, steadying myself by wedging my knee in a crook. "Simeon, are you watching?" I shouted. "I'm about to get all your bread for the week!" Simeon was ignoring me, or trying to, sitting on the steps with the older boys. They were playing poor man's marbles, their pockets filled with pebbles that they'd rubbed against the bricks to get them round as they could.

At this height (about five men with top hats stacked up, maybe) I had a good view of the streets beyond the brick walls. The sun started to slip into blankets of clouds, and the whole city looked washed clean in the pale light. I could see the Y-shaped rivers—the Ohio, the Allegheny, and the Monongahela—sparkling and lots of the roofs of houses beyond. For a moment, it made me wonder whether Momma might still be living inside of one them. Now that she'd rid herself of me and Zach she had more options. Maybe she'd run off to a big city like New York or even out West to pan for gold! Thinking on Momma made me feel like I swallowed burning paper. She could rot. This was my world now and I was going to show that Simeon!

Finally, I got to the last strong limb near the roof and started edging my way out like an inchworm. My hands were icy and damp and my feet kept trying to slip out of my too-big boots. When I was a hand away, I called back down to Simeon so he couldn't deny I'd made it. I could taste his bread now.

"Look, Simeon! I did it!" Just as I reached out to touch the roof line, the branch made a hideous crack beneath me and snapped. I hit near to every limb as I fell, fast as you can say "Pittsburgh, Pennsylvania." Then it all went black.

CHAPTER

When I finally woke up, I wished I hadn't. It felt as if a cow had danced a jig all over my body. Everything hurt except my left arm, which felt like it was missing. It lay beside me like it belonged to somebody else. Zach was there reading the Bible when I woke up. My eyes were so swollen it was easier to keep them closed than open.

"Owen? Owen?" Zach whispered to me. "You've got to get better now."

I groaned but couldn't say anything just yet. I wanted to say I was trying to, but I couldn't make my lips mind my thoughts. I fell back into the black blanket of my mind.

The second time I woke up, it was the middle of the night, the moonlight pouring in through the window, and my brother still beside me, sleeping on the next cot. It was quiet in the small infirmary, nothing like the snoring, coughing, and crying in the boys' dorm upstairs. Even the older boys would sometimes sniffle at night though nobody ever mentioned it come morning, unless he wanted to be blue about the face. My head still hurt, bad—it was a cannonball that I couldn't lift off my pillow.

My stomach started growling so loud I was afraid it might wake Zach. Then again, I knew better than that. At five years older than him, I always tried to protect Zach from the bullies in the neighborhood, and our own pa when he'd come home drunk and riled up. But if I could get Zach to sleep, he never heard a thing— not even Pa and Ma's legendary fights. And after Pa was gone, I don't guess Zach ever heard Momma cry at night either. A blessing.

Next time I woke it was finally morning. It was the gruel that woke me. Hard to believe that tasteless lump could bring me out of sleep, but I felt like I hadn't eaten in a year.

"Zach, can I have some of your mush?"

Zach looked so surprised to see me awake and asking for something I think I scared him.

"How long I been sleeping?"

"Almost four days now. I wondered if you were ever

going to wake up." His voice kind of snagged when he said that last bit, and it made me feel real sorry. He started spooning up his breakfast for me like I was the baby brother. At thirteen it was hard to swallow my pride with the mush.

"I promise I won't do that again," I said, tasting the last bite.

"Owen, even you're not so much a fool to try that again, are you?" Zach asked with a smile.

"No, I mean, I won't brag on myself. It was my mouth that got me into this, not my legs."

"Nah, it was your stomach!" he said, laughing. I couldn't help but start laughing with him though it made my head hurt even worse.

"Well, I promise not to let my stomach talk through my mouth again."

"It's okay, Owen. I'm glad you're talking again."

The nurse walked in then, carrying a tray and her usual scowl. "Well, Owen Burke, I see you are back among the living." She said it without much enthusiasm.

"Yes," I answered, "though my head feels like it might rather be dead."

She came over and touched my forehead with her cool fingers. This reminded me of Momma, and I swallowed back tears from the memory though she probably thought it was the pain.

"Only a demon or an angel could save someone from a fall like that," she said, setting down the tray on a rickety table by the window. When she turned toward me I could feel her studying me, trying to figure out which one I was. Try as I might to be good, I weren't never associated with angels. She slipped her hand behind my neck and pushed me up in the bed. I felt like an axe split my face, square between the eyes. But the hot, bitter tea she made me sip soothed my dry mouth and soon enough took the pain back out the door with her.

It was another seven days before I could walk out of there on my own. Zach stayed with me the whole time, and he never reminded me again about my straw for brains. When they sent me back up to the boys' room, it seemed even sorrier than it had before. It smelled like dirty boys. And dirty boys are mean boys, there just ain't no way around it. My days of hot soup and a generous hunk of bread were over. Hunger returned like a landlord that ain't been paid.

A few days later Miss Eliza and Miss Jane came by to bring rag dolls to the new girls. For new boys, they brought pieces of penny candy, pressing them into their grubby hands. Those sisters didn't realize the bigger kids stole the candy as soon as their backs were turned. Zach and I always called Miss Eliza and Miss

Jane the spinster sisters because they'd never been married, and because they were hard to tell apart with their matching gray hair and dresses. They worked at the orphanage for free most of their days, so we didn't call them that to their faces. They found Zach and me in the corner playing three-in-a-row with pebbles and sticks.

"Why, Owen, how wondrous to see you out of bed!" said Miss Eliza.

"Yes, ma'am."

"How are you feeling?" asked Miss Jane. I think it was Miss Jane—truth is I always got them confused. Like I said, they looked alike and even their smiles seemed to match their plain dresses.

"Better every day," I answered.

"Did they punish you, Owen, for that foolish stunt?" asked Miss Eliza.

"I had to scrub the floor in the boys' dorm." What I didn't mention was that Zach had done the lion's share of the work since my left arm wasn't worth much and the pain was still my companion every time I moved much.

"I hope you learned your lesson, then," Miss Eliza said, crossing her arms and staring down at me sternly.

"Yes'm. I don't reckon on trying to be a squirrel again anytime soon."

Zach laughed though the spinster sisters just pursed their lips as if they'd tasted something sour. Cracking jokes did not show enough regret. Zach said, "Now Owen's stuck in the dirt like a dog!"

"Or an ass!" I countered. "And about as smart."

With that, Zach really lost it. His eight-year-old laugh sounded more like a girl's giggle, and though he tried to swallow it, he just couldn't help himself.

Miss Jane coughed behind her white-gloved hand, obviously trying to stop this nonsense. "Well, how is your arm feeling?" she asked.

"Not at all," I answered, honest, trying to hold back my laughter.

"It's not hurting at all? Isn't that wondrous!" said Miss Eliza. *Wondrous* was a word Miss Eliza couldn't use enough.

"No. I mean, I can't feel it at all," I answered, and demonstrated by lifting my left arm above my head with my good hand and letting go. It fell like a piece of deadwood, landing on my lap.

"Oh, I see," she answered, and then glanced at Miss Jane.

"I'm sure it will get better with time," Miss Eliza said in a singsongy tone. The same voice my momma used to use whenever she lied to us about things getting better.

CHAPTER

THE NEXT DAY Zach and I got word to report to the spinster sisters' cottage. They lived less than a mile from the Home for Destitute and Friendless Youth, and they spent a great many of their hours inside its brick walls. Once a month they invited two children to help them fold and bundle their abolitionist newspaper. I'd never been asked before, and though it was probably pity that got me the invitation, I didn't mind for the chance to taste freedom and perhaps cookies. It was rumored that cookies came with the job. I didn't know how much help I could be with one arm, but I wasn't going to mention that fact and lose Zach's and my chance for an excursion.

The sisters' house was a small three-room cottage, plain as a piece of bread. But you could tell they'd tried to make it look nice by fancying it up with lace curtains and lining the walkway with flowers. They didn't have much furniture except a shiny dining table with carved chairs. On it was the newsletter in fat stacks. Our job was to fold the newsletter into thirds, sort it into stacks of fifty, bind those with twine, and tag them with yellow cards marked with the name of the city they would be delivered to. Zach neatly printed the names of cities I only dreamed of visiting—Philadelphia, Cincinnati, and New York. And while he worked hard at the task, I mainly talked about what we might find in those far-flung places or spied on the boys playing a game of stickball across the street. When the sisters came back in with a tray of cookies, I felt guilty about how small my stack was compared to my brother's. Miss Eliza's disappointment in me was a fresh painting on her face.

When I tasted the cinnamon in the cookies, it reminded me of Momma, and it was hard to swallow the first bite. Momma had always made something with cinnamon to tempt us into studying our letters. She had dreamed of being a schoolteacher instead of a seamstress tied to her machine, and she loved to learn us all she could with whatever snatches of time she could find. Zach read as fine as the rich boys who attended school, but I could sound out most things if I took my time. It was hard to imagine that this time last year we were all still together. Lost in the flavor of home, I ended up eating five whole cookies without even thinking about it. Zach, always good, ate only three.

"Listen to this, Owen," Zach said, pointing to an ad in the paper I hadn't noticed. "Final Notice. Please bring donations of clothing, shoes, and outerwear to the orphanage. The orphan train will depart on March 12, 1853. That's next week!"

"That's thrilling, Zach. Used clothing."

"I don't care about the clothing, Owen, it's the train! The train is coming next week!"

"That train is just an orphanage on wheels." I didn't like Zach's constant talk about heading out West. I was sick of hearing about that train already.

"No! It's our chance to get *out* of an orphanage. To get into a real family again."

"We'll never have a real family again." It was a mean thing to say, and I saw his shoulders slump under my words. I don't know why I had to rip out his excitement, but I didn't want his hopes crushed again. Would someone really want us when our own momma didn't? It was hard to believe. I headed off to the kitchen area, hoping maybe the spinster sisters might offer me a bit of milk instead of the water I would ask for.

I didn't mean to eavesdrop, but when I heard them

say Zach's name, I stopped cold in the doorway. They were washing and drying dishes out of a large basin.

"Zachary is such a beautiful child," said Miss Jane.

"He is sure to be adopted. His countenance is pure," Miss Eliza answered. "But we must face the facts about Owen." I slid to the side so they could not see me even if they turned from their task. What did she mean by face the facts about me?

"He is quite bold and rude," said Miss Jane.

"Nor does he have his brother's fine features," said Miss Eliza. I knew that she was referring to Zach's blond curls and blue eyes, which were just like our momma's. I had the darker skin, hair, and eyes of our pa.

"You know those older boys will be expected to earn their keep," Miss Eliza said. "One who can eat more than he can help will not find a home."

"I know. But it's not fair. They're orphans, not work-horses or slaves!" Miss Jane answered. You could tell it had been a topic they'd discussed before.

"Now, sister, you cannot compare slavery to the work that farm boys must do," Miss Eliza admonished.

"I know, I know. I just hate to think of our Zachary breaking his back out in those fields," said Miss Jane.

"He is not *our* Zachary, sister. And he would do well to know a decent father." Though Eliza was right about my father, it pained me to hear someone say it aloud.

"But what if no one adopts him because of Owen?"

"We shall cross that bridge if it appears," Miss Eliza answered.

"You mean *when* it appears. Because it surely will," said Miss Jane.

"Wouldn't it be wondrous to adopt them ourselves?" asked Miss Eliza.

"Don't be silly, sister. We don't know the first thing about raising a boy," Miss Jane answered.

"Well, at least we can volunteer for the orphan train and see for ourselves," Miss Eliza said, her voice sounding sad.

"It is the least we can do, sister," answered Miss Eliza.

I backed away silently and headed to the outhouse. My thoughts were a stew of emotion—hate for my father, shame for my worthless arm, anger at Momma. Worst of all, guilt bubbled to the top. I hated the words I'd heard from the spinster sisters, but I knew the cold truth of their words. Zach's only hope for a real family was without me.

CHAPTER

FOR THE NEXT SIX DAYS I pretended that the orphan train was the best thing since cookies were invented. Oh, I talked it up. Mostly in lies. I didn't know much about the trains, not really. I knew they were the fan-dangled idea of some New Yorker who hated seeing homeless kids in prison. He thought they could find homes out West with families who could use an extra pair of hands on the farm—free labor. And since lots of families lost kids to fevers or accidents, most had room for a new one, or leastways this was the thinking.

'Course that ain't what I told Zach. I told him they served fancy foods and that families from far and wide came to pick their kids from the orphan train 'cause they were supposed to be the cream on the clabber. Told him they handed out candy at each stop, and musicians and posture masters came on board just to entertain the children between cities. When he asked me why I'd had such a change of heart, I told him that I'd heard all about it while spying at the spinster sisters' house. He believed me, of course, which only made me feel worse about my plan. I figured since I wasn't bragging on my own self, that I wasn't breaking my promise to him either. Hell, that train sounded like a fair and a parade rolled into one when I laid out my words.

When train day finally came, the Ladies' Society showed up at daybreak to make sure that each child got a haircut and a bath in clean water. I don't think I had ever seen my toes in the bottom of a bathtub before. I usually bathed in a mud soup. This time the water could almost be considered warm, though the soap still burned my scratches like fire.

Then the spinster sisters handed out crisp white shirts and new pants to the boys. We also got nice warm wool socks with no holes and new shoes that were just a hair too big. They took our old clothes and burned them in rusty barrels out back. The girls got new dresses and fancy ribbons for their hair. I even got a nice bandana for my sling. I preferred my arm, still numb as the day I woke up, tucked inside the sling instead of just dangling useless by my leg.

After I was dressed in my new clothes, I came up and stood behind Zach in the mirror as he combed out what was left of his blond curls. We looked like one of the fancy daguerreotypes they take downtown. I wished I could have one of us to keep for always. Even Momma's face seemed more like a dream sometimes. I tried not to think on my pa's face 'cause that was one memory I wanted to forget.

"Ain't you excited?" Zach asked me.

"I am." I tried to match his voice, but mine sounded high and false. Luckily Zach didn't seem to notice.

"Maybe we'll get adopted by rich people out on a farm where we can each have our own horse!" He sounded younger than eight with his voice so excited.

"Maybe, Zach, maybe."

"We'll get lots of food and get to go to school."

"Get to go to school? You mean *have* to go to school." Now I sounded like the baby brother, not him. I'd never been much on school.

"A real school, Owen, not like they do here at the orphanage." He smiled up at me, and I thought about abandoning my plan. I could take my chances and stay with him or at least see that he got to a good family first. But I knew it'd never work. Zach wouldn't go with a family that didn't want me, too.

I started to hug him but I didn't want to make him

suspicious, so I messed up his perfect hair instead. Then I went to get our bundles for the train.

"Now, why'd you go and do that, Owen?" he yelled after me.

"'Cause you're my little brother," I yelled back at him, and then added, "and you always will be."

"I know that!" He rolled his eyes at me and stuck out his tongue.

The train came right at dusk. The plan was to get the children to sleep through the longest part of the journey and begin placing children with families come morning. It was an odd arrangement, to be sure, setting off when most kids would get tucked into bed.

It was starting to rain and there were too many of us to fit under the roofline of the depot. We looked like some kind of sad army all lined up on the platform, our white shirts plastering to our skin beneath. Most of the kids were young. The spinster sisters held some in their arms, those who were too small to even walk. Everybody had a cardboard name tag pinned to his or her shirt. I filled out Zach's tag for him in my best printing. On the back I penned, "Owen Burke's brother." I attached it to his shirt and told him not to touch it.

Inside, the crowded train car smelled like wet wool and lye soap. The kids were too excited to settle down.

Some were singing songs, babies were crying, new walkers fussing. I was nervous trying to time my escape at just the right moment. Too soon and they'd realize I was gone and wait for me. Too late and I would never get off. As the train started to pull away from the station, I made my move.

"I've got to make water." My last words for my brother would forever remind him of an outhouse, I thought. Slipping past the spinster sisters was easier than I imagined, their attention nabbed by a baby who was wailing for her bottle. But I was glad they had decided to chaperone so's they could keep an eye on Zach for me. Only Simeon noticed me, and I could feel the heat of his eyes follow me as I shuffled to the back of the car. I pretended like I was going to sit down with Rebekkah Dobson, a girl who managed to stay heavy even in the orphanage, and Simeon soon lost interest. When he did, I bolted to the brass handle of the door and nearly ran smack into a porter.

"Where you going, son?" he asked me.

"Need some air, feeling a bit puny," I answered, and for once I was telling the truth.

He moved out of my way. I guess there's nothing adults hate more than vomit.

"Take your time, but don't lean too far out over the rail out there, you hear me?"

"Yes, sir," I answered politely, and he moved inside the car and as far away from me as possible. I climbed down the three stairs and jumped off the train into the inky, rainy night. I tumbled into a patch of sticker bushes and landed on my bad arm, slicing me with pain all the way to my fingertips. Now Zach had a chance for a real home, without me.

CHAPTER

I CIRCLED AROUND THE TRAIN DEPOT and away from the orphanage. I had a small bag that I made out of a flour sack and sewed a piece a twine in the top with a needle. It was right ugly, but inside I had saved my bread for near a week. When I took out the rubbish, I'd managed to pinch a slab of cheese from the wheel of it in the kitchen too. Both made a thudding rhythm as I walked, though I wished there was some coins in there to jangle, but I had none. The cheese and bread would be like soup in the rain, so I stuffed them under my coat and continued on. The rain pelted me as I walked past large brick factories and apartment buildings, small cottages and fancy houses for rich people.

It seemed the longer I walked, the more people joined me, which was odd, especially with the rain pouring down in buckets. I worried, at first, that someone might recognize me, but in the pouring rain everyone was too concerned with staying dry and getting somewhere.

The water dripped off the large brims of the women's bonnets and umbrellas like a porch, but they were better off than the men whose top hats forced the cold water square onto their shoulders. Women and men in plainer clothes tried to stay dry underneath tents of newspaper they held over their heads. It didn't much help. But despite the downpour the crowd seemed as excited as the children on the orphan train. When we turned the corner, I could finally see why.

Tied up on the river was the most gigantic boat I'd ever seen. It made the other boats look like little toys, and stretched longer than a city block. More than four times as long as any other boat and twice as high, I swear it! If a fairy-tale king come riding out of the front doors on a white horse, why it would not have surprised me. It was shining bright white even in the dark rain. Red letters edged with what looked like gold spelled out *River Palace* across the side of the boat.

A band was playing lively music and people's steps kept time with the drum. The women giggled together like girls, men pointed at the intricate designs in the wood, and I heard a couple marvel that something so huge could stay afloat. And everybody moved straight toward the wide front doors that looked like an open mouth, including me.

"Welcome to the *River Palace*! Be the first to enjoy the deluxe theater on our opening night! Only fifty cents to see clowns, a scene from Shakespeare's *Hamlet*, and trained exotic animals!"

When men started collecting tickets and coins, I finally woke up. I couldn't believe it. It was a circus—a whole circus—on the *inside* of that boat! A floating circus! If I hadn't been there to see it, I'd think whoever was telling me about it was the biggest liar in all of these United States.

A man with whiskey on his breath shoved me aside; he reeked just like my pa used to. Pushed out of the crowd, I walked alongside that beautiful boat on the muddy bank. It looked like the whole city of Pittsburgh had come out for the opening. There musta been thousands who filed through the doors. Finally, the music stopped. The plank was empty now, all the money men gone inside. Only one old Negro was trying to sweep the mud off the deck. He glanced at me, so I turned to leave. He looked meaner than my pa with no drink.

"Did you lose your ticket?" the Negro man asked me.

"I ain't had one."

"No. I don't guess you look much like you did."

He put his head back down to his work and continued on, ignoring me. I hadn't ever spoken directly to a Negro before, though I'd seen some. I'd surely never seen one alone before. This one looked old, his hair mostly white and his face full of lines. He didn't look much like he'd ever smiled.

"Where's the steam engine? Is it under the water?" I asked, curiosity making me bold. His head snapped up. The whites of his eyes looked yellow in the gaslight.

"You're pretty smart to notice there's no engine." He stared at me, his hand resting on the top of the wide broom.

"How she get around, then? They couldn't have just made her for Pittsburgh or they would've built an amphitheater, not a boat."

"Like I said, you're smart," said the man, motioning me to follow him. It wasn't something I'd ever heard anyone say to me before. I walked up the rest of the plank and put my foot on the ship itself. My heart somersaulted to be on board. "They use the *Attaboy*," he said, pointing to a small boat down the shore a bit. "It's a side-wheeler with all the muscle."

"Imagine that! Something that puny pushing this up the river. What about that one?" I asked, pointing to an even smaller paddleboat painted similiar to the others.

"Yup. That's the *Hummingbird*. It goes ahead of the *Palace* and plasters towns in paper."

"Putting up the fancy posters and such?" I was dying to know everything about this circus all of a sudden.

"Yes, that's right," he answered.

"And is this one of Dan Rice's famous shows?"

"No. It's Hathaway's show." A little disappointment pinched me. Dan Rice was a world-famous clown I'd longed to see. Why, I bet anyone would recognize his mug from circus posters even more than the new president!

The man stopped sweeping for a second and asked me, "What's your name?"

"Owen Burke. What's yours?"

"They call me Solomon," he said, though he did not offer his hand. "Well, Owen Burke, would you like a peek at the show?"

When my face split open in a smile, he laughed. "Follow me, then."

CHAPTER

SOLOMON PUT ME IN A SPYING SPOT under a stair-well that only someone who worked on the circus would know about. I could see near everything except one small slice of the ring. An equestrian somersaulted front ways and back while the horse underneath him kept a steady gallop. The crowd kept count each time he did it and with each number they got a bit louder. When they reached twenty-one, the man took a bow on his horse and exited behind a heavy red curtain.

Next, a dignified-looking man wearing tall riding boots, a short, suede jacket, and a bow tie strode into the ring. "Ladies and Gentlemen, now you shall see a stupendous act none have witnessed before."

The band struck up a sprightly tune while two big men pushed a giant cage on wheels into the center of the ring. Inside crouched an enormous black bear wearing a beaded vest. Beside him stood a beautiful woman pressed against the bars like she'd been captured by the beast. Her hair was scarlet and curly and nearly matched her glittery costume, which had a skirt that ended just above her knees. I gasped to see this woman alone with such a ferocious beast, but I clapped my hand over my mouth, hoping no one had heard me. The audience, too, sucked in their breath and then a hush fell over the auditorium, everyone riveted to this amazing scene.

"Welcome Zelda Bouclaire and Titus the Russian Bear!"

People seemed too stunned to clap. Zelda climbed down from her perch and picked up a rider's whip and tapped the bear right on the tip of his nose. He lumbered up onto a painted stand. When Zelda raised her arms above her head, the bear imitated her.

"Thank you for being so quiet," she said to the audience with an exotic accent. "My bear, Titus, is a bit shy with crowds." Then the bear covered his eyes with his paws like he really was bashful! The whole audience erupted in laughter.

"Titus, would you like some of that lemonade our patrons are enjoying?"

The bear shook his head.

"Perhaps you'd prefer some roasted chestnuts, then? The audience seems to love them!"

Just mentioning the nuts made my mouth water. I hadn't eaten a thing since breakfast and my stomach answered me now. I put a hand on my stomach to ease the rumble and saw a pair of boots slow down behind me. I held my breath and tried to scrunch down and make myself small. What would they do with me if I got caught? Finally, the *kachoink-kachoink* of the boots moved along, and I was able to focus my attention again on Zelda and her bear.

Titus was now down on his knees, his paws together and his head lowered as if he was praying. The audience laughed again, but it was gentler, like they were watching a show their own grandkids were putting on for them. They never took their eyes away from Zelda and her bear, though the duo did trick after trick for a good ten minutes more. Finally she told him it was time to clean up his mess.

Fetching toys like a baby, Titus picked up an enormous orange rattle, his large blue-and-white striped ball, and bear-sized alphabet blocks. When he was done, he stood next to her and they held hands and bowed together. The people stood up and clapped, whistled, and called out for Zelda and Titus. I would've stood up and cheered with them if I could. I shifted onto my knees to get one last glimpse of the bear as the cage was being rolled back out, when a large hand grabbed hold of my shoulder and pulled me right out of my hiding spot. My face felt like someone had slapped me and fear roped itself around my ribs. I was used to being in trouble at the orphanage, but this felt dangerous. The man had me by the scruff of my neck and shoved me when I tried to drag my feet. I tried to form some excuses, but my mind was an empty bucket that no words would fill.

"Hey, boss, look at this rat I found underneath the stairs," the man said, giving me one last shove that pitched me so I lost my balance and landed on one knee.

Looking up from the deck I felt like a dog before his master. But this boss who hurried over to us was a man no bigger than a ten-year-old girl. He took off his tall top hat, revealing a shiny bald head. His piercing gray eyes looked like they might burn me.

Finally my voice found me again. "I only wanted a peek. I didn't mean no harm—"

"Drown it." He interrupted my excuse making without emotion and turned on the heel of his shiny leather boot. Another man grabbed my feet and I was pitched into the Allegheny River like trash.

CHAPTER

7

WITH MY ARM STILL WRAPPED in my sling, I slipped under the brown waters. March is no time to be swimming, I can tell you that. It felt like a million icy needles were poking into my skin, and my ears felt like they might shatter and fall right off. I tried to swim, but my boots filled with water and weighed me down like bricks. Even though my feet scraped the mud, it was too slippery to get a purchase on it. As I started to float past the boat, panic ripped through me. I did not want to die. Zach's face slipped into my mind as I went under the black waters again and again.

Just when I thought I'd end up being fish food, a long stick poked me in the ribs as I struggled to the surface. I grabbed on to it with my good hand and wrapped my legs around it, too. Relief and hope filled in the spaces where panic ruled. Following the white pole up to the top I was able to see who was trying to save me. It was Solomon—the Negro who'd snuck me into the show. It seemed like forever before I was near enough for Solomon to reach over and help me to climb over the railing. Just as I landed in a giant puddle of relief on the deck, the little man came around the corner with the two who had thrown me in.

"Solomon! Why have you brought this rubbish aboard?" he demanded, his fists on his hips. He stopped short just in front of me.

Solomon dropped his head and looked at the owner's boots. They were so shiny I could see the shape of Solomon's face in them.

"Sorry, Mr. Hathaway. I saw him drowning," Solomon answered, just above a whisper.

"Serves him right for sneaking onto my boat."

Solomon's head snapped up and he looked right at Mr. Hathaway, surprised by this news.

"Should we pitch him back in the water, Mr. Hathaway?" asked the bigger of the two men, starting toward me.

"Just get him off my boat," said Hathaway. "I don't like trash on it."

The big man yanked me by my bad arm and I was suddenly on my feet being shoved once again to shore. At least I wasn't going in the water this time.

"Wait," Solomon said quietly. "I've got an idea."

"What did you say?" Hathaway demanded.

"I said I've got an idea, sir," Solomon answered, looking in Hathaway's face this time.

"Oh, you do, do you? Did you hear that, boys? Solomon has got himself an idea!" Hathaway laughed like he was watching a clown performing inside the circus ring, only his laugh was peppered with cruelty instead of joy. The other men chuckled, though it was hard to tell if they thought it was funny or if they were just trying to make their boss happy.

"Well, let's hear this big idea, Solomon," Hathaway said, crossing his arms in front of his silky blazer.

"Yes, sir," Solomon answered, stepping up closer to the boss. "I was thinking he could pay for his ticket."

I started coughing when he said that 'cause I didn't have even a penny, never mind enough for a circus ticket on a fancy floating boat! There's no way I could pay for it. What was Solomon thinking?

"Yes. What a perfectly reasonable idea, Solomon. He should just pay for his ticket." Hathaway busted up laughing then, slapping one of the men on the back. "Why, he should get himself some lemonade and a bag of roasted nuts, too!" he said, looking at the other men, waiting for them to laugh with him. They obliged, though this time you could tell they were just trying to please the boss.

"No, I mean . . ." Solomon tried to explain, but the three men kept laughing, louder than they needed to be. Finally Solomon got out the rest of his words when the men bent over trying to get air. "He can work for me is what I mean."

"Oh, I see, now you're hiring a staff, are you?" said Hathaway. The other men laughed outrageously again. Mr. Hathaway's face sobered up now, though it seemed smeared with red jam. Whether he was angry or what I didn't know, but it made me uneasy. I decided to stare at the tips of my waterlogged boots. It was hard for me to concentrate on what they were saying, because I was racked with chills and my teeth were clattering like I'd been in an icebox.

"No, sir. But we could use another pair of hands for cleaning," Solomon said, pointing at all the mud and muck plastered to the deck of the boat.

"I don't suspect his momma would appreciate us taking him downriver," said the larger man. Never mind he had just tried to kill me in the selfsame river.

I piped up with that. "I've got no parents, sir. I'd be a hard worker, I promise. And I don't eat much."

Hathaway looked me over from head to foot then and nearly lit my stomach on fire with the intensity of his gray stare. "I suspect you have not had the *opportunity* to eat much, not that you *don't*."

"He could bunk with me," Solomon offered.

"Get him off my deck, then," Mr. Hathaway said, dismissing us both.

"Yes, sir," Solomon answered.

"Thank you, sir. You won't regret it," I said, offering my hand, which he ignored.

"See that I don't, or next time you won't get pulled out."

Solomon led me around to the back door. He threw a horse blanket around my shoulders, and I followed him into the bowels of the ship. Behind the fancy halls and auditorium was a homely structure for the performers. Though everything was new, it was not made to impress but to function. There were no fancy paintings or velvet curtains, just whitewashed walls and hooks, shelves and poles that held every manner of costume, tool, or prop. It was dim, with just a single gaslight in a plain glass case to show the way. After weaving our way through a maze of hallways and closets, we arrived at where the performers were getting ready to go in the ring.

Their costumes looked surprisingly awkward and

homemade without the bright gaslights and crystal chandeliers to sparkle off of them. The bold stripes of color on their cheekbones and eyes looked harsh. The few performers who bothered to turn their heads in my direction frowned as if I were a drowned rat scuttling through them. But I didn't care. I was happy to be aboard, and alive. My legs wobbled like the bones inside them were replaced with licorice. Only where Solomon's hand rested on my shoulder did my body have any warmth in it.

Some of the horses poked their heads out of their stalls as we walked by. Solomon rolled open the last door. A pile of clean hay was heaped on one side of the dark stall. In the corner I noticed a bedroll and a lantern hanging on a wooden peg.

"This'll be home. Now you best get off them wet clothes and warm up or I shouldn't of bothered to pull you out of the river."

I could only nod, with my teeth chattering so. As I tried to unbutton my shirt with the frozen, shaky fingers of my good hand, Solomon went and fetched me several horse blankets. He rolled out his own bedroll and then handed me a nightshirt—his own, I supposed—and though it swallowed me, I didn't complain. He picked up my drenched clothes and walked out without another word. I wrapped myself in the scratchy brown wool from head to toe and piled the extra blankets on top.

It took a long time for my body to stop aching and twitching. Through the walls I could hear the audience's applause and cheering, the orchestra, and the pounding hooves of the animals. It felt like I had been snatched up and dropped inside somebody else's dream. I thought about Zach for the first time in hours, and I wondered where he might be. Maybe he'd already been chosen by a new family and was sitting at a table with other kids and a mom and dad who wanted him. I ached to tell him about all I'd seen and what happened to me. I imagined all he might say, and it was like another blanket, the sound of his voice in my mind.

CHAPTER

I MUST'VE FALLEN ASLEEP, because the next thing I knew, Solomon was shaking me awake.

"Come on, now. You got to get up," he said none too gently. I didn't remember where I was for a second, or how I'd gotten here. It must've shown in my face, too, because Solomon said, "You're on the *River Palace*. And there's plenty of work to be done. Now get dressed." Yesterday I was nothing but an orphan boy with no hope for a home or real prospects; now here I was an employee of the greatest river circus! A body just never could account for what might happen. I jumped out of the pallet ready to prove myself to Solomon or Hathaway or whoever need be.

Solomon handed me a bundle of clothes, and though they weren't mine, I put them on without question.

They were a little bit small for me, the pants barely reaching my ankles, but at least they were dry and warm. I even had a pair of boots, though I had to curl my toes a bit to get them on.

"Your things aren't dry yet," Solomon said simply, and then motioned for me to follow him. He led me to the first horse stall and gave me a pitchfork and a wheelbarrow. He pointed to the soiled hay. He helped me fill the first barrowful and then showed me to the river stable, as he called it. It looked like just another stable door, but when it slid open, there was the river lapping just under the tips of your boots. Solomon dumped the horse mess overboard with a single shove.

We'd been city people. My pa had worked as a tailor before he'd found the bottle. Momma was fine with a needle too, and she was always chained to her machine to make extra money. I'd never rode on a horse, though I'd seen the back of many from wagons and buggies. They sure made a mess. Cleaning up after them was hard work, especially with just one arm. I had to wedge the pitchfork under my armpit and grip it down near the blades, then balance the weight on my knee to dump it into the barrow. Solomon came back to check on me just as I was starting on the second stall.

"Were you born with that useless left arm?" he asked, watching my balancing act.

"No. I busted it just a few weeks ago, falling out of a tree."

"Let me see."

I walked over and faced Solomon. He moved his thick, calloused hands up and down my arm and behind my shoulder. Though all my old bruises were finally faded into a dull yellow, I yelped when he pressed behind my shoulder blade.

"Follow me," Solomon said, leading me into a large closet that had a dozen shelves on each wall. A table was chained to the floor. Bottles of every shape, size, and color lined the shelves. Some contained leaves or stalks of plants, while others were filled with dark, murky liquids. Drawn onto the labels were intricate pictures but no words.

"Take off that shirt."

While I unbuttoned with my good hand, Solomon pulled down three different jars and began grinding the stalk of one plant in a large bowl with a stone pestle. Then he added some bluish liquid and some black liquid and mixed it all up with his hands. It smelled putrid.

"Come here," he said. I did what he said though I didn't want to.

"What is that?" I asked.

"A poultice. It will help your arm heal." A look of annoyance crossed his face.

"I don't know if it will make it heal, but it sure will make it stink!" I laughed, and thumped the table with my good hand, trying to get a reaction.

"You don't much smell like strawberries now," he said with a slow smile.

"No, sir, I don't guess I do," I answered, glad to see that Solomon was capable of smiling. He had seemed much like a tree trunk until now.

"Don't call me 'sir,'" Solomon said, spreading the paste onto my shoulder and down my arm. It made my eyes sting, and it felt hot as he rubbed it into my skin.

"Why not?" I asked. I'd been hit upside the back of my head so many times for not saying it to my pa that now it came automatic, like closing your eyes when you sneeze.

"'Cause a Negro ain't no 'sir' in this world. Even a free one." Solomon's dark eyes narrowed and he stared straight through to my bones. I dropped my head and stared at the tips of my scuffed boots.

"Are you free?" I asked. Hathaway had treated him like a slave, so I'd just assumed that's what he was. It never occurred to me that he could be anything else but a slave.

"I have my papers."

"Oh." I didn't know what else to say, and Solomon didn't say anything more. He wrapped my arm with a clean rag; then he buttoned up my shirt for me. I guess he'd noticed how long it took me earlier. A bell rang in the distance, breaking the silence.

"What's that for?" I asked

"Time for breakfast."

These were the nicest words I had heard in days.

"Yes, sir. I mean, yes, Solomon, let's eat!" Solomon laughed at that and started to clap me on the shoulder but then dropped his hand.

We walked through the heavy red curtains into the circus ring. It was strange to be down on this level and see the rows and rows of carved chairs and balcony seats all empty. It looked almost haunted. Dozens of tables had been set up around the ring. The performers sat together at one end, the workmen on the other, and the Negro workers at their own table, out in the hall. There was a buffet line set out with more food than I'd ever seen in one place.

Puffy biscuits were piled in pyramids, and a giant pot held more than a bucketful of gravy. Crisp bacon and sausage links shared a large platter. Three different colors of fruit were all cut up in triangles. Even pastries with cherry filling and creamy vanilla icing waited for anyone to pick them. While we stood in the world's longest line, my stomach howled so loud it made Solomon turn around. Waiting at the orphanage sometimes took a long time, but it never mattered since the food was so awful. But this was the most amazing display I'd ever seen in my entire life, and I couldn't wait to get to it.

I loaded my plate with four biscuits swimming in gravy, three pieces of bacon and two sausage links. I took a cherry pastry, too, like a dessert. I hoped Mr. Hathaway would not get a view of my plate. He was right—if given the opportunity I'd eat like a hog. I followed Solomon to the table. He turned around, surprised to see me behind him.

"You can't sit here, Owen."

"But I don't know nobody else. Besides, we share a room. Can't we share a table?"

Solomon shook his head in exasperation.

"All right, then," he said finally and put down his plate. I set my plate down across from him and next to the oldest woman I'd ever seen. Her hair was white, white as the paint on the ship, and her face was covered, every bit of it, with lines and crevices like a map.

"This is Miss Jasmine," said Solomon. The woman looked up at me but didn't smile. She just nodded and put her face back to her plate.

"Hello, ma'am."

She nodded at me again as she ate her biscuits, slow, like it was hard for her to chew. Then she reached over and patted my hand and smiled. She was the oldest person I'd ever seen, and I wondered if she could talk.

"Can she talk?" I whispered to Solomon.

She must've heard me then 'cause she snorted loud and started laughing behind her hand.

"Lord, yes, honey, I can talk." She cackled again, shaking her head. "They bought me to talk!"

"Really?" I asked, wondering what in the world an old slave woman would talk about that Hathaway would pay to buy her.

"People come from far and wide to hear me," she answered, her eyes dancing, obviously still amused by my ignorance.

"She was the nursemaid to George Washington himself," Solomon explained.

"She was?" I asked, impressed to be next to anyone who would've known Washington, even as a boy. The whole table fell apart then, laughing at me. My face felt bright red and my ears huge.

"Don't you feel bad now, son," the old woman said, smiling. "We haven't had a first of May in a few years to pick on, is all."

"What's a first of May?" I asked.

"Somebody new to the circus," she answered.

"Why do they call them that?"

"'Cause that's when the wagons would set out on

tour for the year, on the first day of May," she said, and winked at me.

"Oh," I said, not really caring what they called me as long as I got to eat this much food. All my questions and concerns dropped from my mind when I picked up my fork. It was more food than I'd had in a month. The gravy on the biscuits even had real hunks of sausage floating in it. The biscuits melted with each bite, they were so soft and fresh.

"You need to slow down or you're going to get yourself sick," said Solomon.

I looked up to see everybody at the table staring at me like I was a starving stray dog. I tried to swallow the mouthful of food, but my throat felt tight. My ears, too, felt hot with shame. For the rest of the meal I made myself count to four between bites, though I just wanted to keep shoveling it in, afraid it might disappear like any good thing in the orphanage did. I ate every bit of everything on my plate and drank two glasses of buttermilk besides. I'd shovel horse dirt every day of my life if they fed me like this.

CHAPTER

"We've got to get ready for the first show," Solomon said.

"I thought that's what I've been doing all morning," I answered from my hands and knees where I'd been scrubbing. My right arm felt like it weighed a hundred pounds, and my back like an elephant had sat on it. Solomon reached down and hooked me under the shoulder, but when he pulled me up it made me squeal since he had me under my bad arm.

"Sorry, Owen, I didn't mean to hurt you."

"I know, Solomon."

"You've got to stop babying that arm and get your strength back in it. You can't just tuck it away in that baby blanket and expect it to start working again."

"It's useless, so what does it matter?" I asked him.

"Who told you it was useless? A doctor?" he asked, his hands on his hips, almost like my momma used to do when she was angry at us kids.

"No. I just figured if something could've been done, it would've."

"Who spends money on an orphan's arm?" he asked again. He was full of questions. He grabbed the bucket of wax and started heading toward the supply closet. I followed.

"What do you mean?" I asked, having to walk double time to keep up with Solomon's long stride.

"Even a slave is worth more," he answered, his face a stone. "Like a mule."

I disagreed with him. "People ain't animals."

"To some they are. See here. If a slave breaks down, then cotton don't get picked and sent off to market. That's dollars straight out of the master's pocket."

"But if an orphan gets hurt, the only one it hurts is himself," I said, putting two and two together.

"Exactly. Now, come on, we don't have a lot of time left." He put the wax bucket and rags back in the closet and started out again.

"What do we have to do?"

"You'll see."

We spent the last couple of hours shining everything a ticketholder might touch while they were at the circus—doorknobs and banisters and the chairs. Every upholstered chair had wooden arms—and there were thousands of them, hundreds on each level—and we wiped them down to a shine. All the gas lanterns had to have the grime rubbed off. Then we repeated the same tasks over on the *Attaboy*, too. The most difficult task was cleaning the giant letters down the side of the boat. Solomon tied a rope around my waist so I wouldn't fall in the river again, and I leaned out each of the twenty-four windows to scrub off the mud and bird droppings that marred the words *River Palace*.

An hour before the show we were down on the hippodrome track again, cleaning up the last of the animal mess. The hippodrome track was on the outside of the performance circle, and it could get mighty full of animal mess. Sawdust was barreled out and we raked it smooth. I didn't put my arm back in my sling like Solomon said. Instead I tried to rest it on the rake handle while I was working. When my arm started to fall, Solomon tore my sling into strips and tied my hand to the handle of the rake or shovel. It was awkward, but if I concentrated all my thoughts down the one hand, my fingers could grip the slick wood beneath it.

After that we did the strangest thing ever. Solomon laid several wood circles over the fresh sawdust in the outer ring. Then he sprinkled chalk dust around each one. It was like a stencil I'd seen a sign painter use once. After each circle was outlined, he picked up the stencil and carefully put a letter or number inside it. It was an easy task and I started helping. Soon the whole outer circle was littered with circles. Curiosity got the best of me when he didn't offer up any explanation.

"You've got to tell me, Solomon!" I said, about to burst with not knowing.

"Tell you what?" He seemed amused by my outburst.

"What are we doing this for?"

"Oh, this," he said, and chuckled to himself. "It's another way for Hathaway to make money, is all."

"How?"

"People puts bets down on the circles. If some horse or elephant dung lands inside their circle during the opening parade of animals, then they get free lemonade or nuts for the show."

"They bet on crap?" I asked, unbelieving.

"In a manner of speaking." He laughed behind his hand.

"Huh. Who would've thought to make money off animal dirt?"

"Hathaway. He could make money off anything," he said.

"Probably even lice," I offered.

"Ha!" he said, and slapped his knee. "I bet you're right about that!"

I shook my head and finished the circles. Lord, this place was the opposite of the orphanage. For one, the food was amazing. Best, though, was that there was always something to look at—fancy paintings, freaks, or wild animals. When I thought about the orphanage, I thought of white—the walls, the furniture, heck, most of the food was white too. On the *River Palace* everything blazed with color and sound. Deep red and purple fabrics at the windows and on the chairs, gold tassels, and shiny costumes colored like candy. Beasts roaring or trumpeting, the pounding of hooves, all sounds that filled my days. My favorites were the spritely tunes that the orchestra practiced while we worked, giving a rhythm to tasks that would seem miserable otherwise.

It was exciting to see the circus come to life. It made me feel important, like I was a part of something, and it kept me from thinking too much on Zach. The performers shed their everyday clothes and put on their fancy jeweled costumes. Sparkling blankets and saddles were strapped to each horse, and plumes were fastened between their ears. The performers applied layers of makeup to their faces; even the men lined their eyes and put color on their cheeks. When

I stared for a moment too long, Solomon explained it was so the audience even at the top could see their expressions.

As the boat filled with patrons, things got more hectic. All the circus performers lined up, readying themselves for the parade around the track. The animals, the equestrians, the acrobats and oddities, all looked like something out of a fairy tale, but no one smiled until they went through the curtains, in front of the guests. By far the most fascinating part was the wild animals. There were two ostriches with leashes and saddles, and a baby elephant whose trunk seemed to be in constant motion, like she was looking for something she could never quite find.

Titus, the Russian bear, was pulled out in a cage carved with scenes from Goldilocks. It made me think of my momma and how she used to tell us tales just before bed. The next cage was even larger, painted bloodred, and inside were three large lions. The heavy paws of the lions made a *skitch, skitch* sound as they paced around the cage. Long poles hooked into the cages and heavily muscled Negro men pushed the lions into the ring.

A heavy drumroll signaled the start of the parade. As the performers all moved toward the sounds of the excited audience, Solomon led me to the permanent animal stalls and cages. During the show, I was to clean them and fill each one with fresh water, straw, and food. The animals would be hungry after the performance, but they were to get only a bit of food at a time. If they were completely satisfied, they'd never work for their trainers, and they had a second performance to go yet. I was sore disappointed not to see even a slice of the show, but surely someday soon I'd get to see it from the top. I kept telling myself that, anyway, as I stared at the mounds and mounds of animal dirt. I could hear the muffled calls of the ringmaster, so to amuse myself I thought about what I would say to an audience about the work before me:

Ladies and gentlemen! Witness Owen Burke,
The great master of mammoth mounds of animal dirt!
Be astonished! Amazed! Amused!

I kept this up until I finished the lions' cage, and then my hands followed the rhythm of the music through the walls until the cages began filling with their tenants again. Lunch and dinner both were two biscuits with thick ham slices tucked between and an apple all stuffed into my mouth quick as I could, leaning on my rake. Then it was straight back to work cleaning the theater and mucking the stalls. After the second performance the meat eaters would get their biggest meal of the day, and I hoped to see them take it. But during their feeding time Solomon and I had to sweep and polish the main deck so that it would be clean for the next day's performances.

Solomon told me that in big cities like Cincinnati, we might have three shows a day instead of two. It was hard to believe anyone could work any harder than we were already. When the boat was finally unhitched from the shore and the tugboats began pulling her like a sled up a hill, I finally got to collapse on my pallet in the stall, too tired for thoughts or daydreams. I woke once in the night to the strange calls and rumblings of the animals, which made me dream I was being hunted by the beasts. But after my heart stopped racing, the noises became a sort of strange lullaby that sure beat the heck out of the coughing and crying the orphanage held, though I missed Zach's cold toes.

CHAPTER

10

THE DAYS SLIPPED BY in an endless routine of work and sleep. Every morning before the sun cracked the sky, Solomon would shake me awake and press me into a task. At night the boat would travel along the river and we'd wake up in some new town. It didn't matter because I only left the boat to fetch water, and that was always so early no one was much about. It didn't matter none to me because if we weren't there on a Lord's Day, I never got to see any of it anyway. So it was only when I scrubbed the great painted words from the windows during the day did I catch a glimpse of the lives that continued on shore without knowledge of me.

I know it was stupid, but if I got the chance I'd scan the crowd of kids that always ended up on the banks staring at the *Palace*. The old-timers called them "lot lice" 'cause they show up and stick around without buying a ticket. I knew chances of Zach being on a river town and heading into the South was small, but I kept studying the lot lice just the same, hoping to glimpse his fair face or a patch of his blond curls.

We didn't have shows on Sundays, for it was against the law most everywhere. It was a fine thing too—everyone needed a day of rest, even the animals. Lord Hathaway (he had recently given himself that title) handed out the money himself after the final performance of the week. Most workers headed straight into town and blew it on gambling, beer, and fancy foods. Solomon stashed his money in a leather pouch he wore around his neck, and I never saw him spend but for an occasional bag of stale candied nuts that was only a nickel for us anyway.

I got twenty-five cents each week, which was my take after they figured out what I owed for room and board. I wondered if I was paid the same as a worker who had a real bed since I still slept on straw, but of course I didn't say anything for fear that Hathaway would throw me overboard for running my mouth. Of course, most workers had two good arms to use while I had one. What I wanted to buy with my money was a ticket to the show. But every time a show was running I was too busy cleaning up what comes out the back of the animals to even catch a glimpse of the front.

I'd found my own spectacle to watch. Come Sunday, I'd tuck the quarter in my pocket and climb up to my favorite place on the whole ship—the roof. It was flat on top, but it was also hot in the sun, so most people didn't like it, or had never climbed the skinny ladder up to find out what was there. It was quiet, and the view was always amazing and different.

Some days the brown river looked like a snake slithering through the trees, the sun glinting off the tips of the waves like scales down her back. I liked to lay back with my hands under my head and soak up the warm blanket of the sun. And every Sunday I'd make a prayer for Zach that he was safe and warm and in a real school, just like he wanted. I did not regret jumping from the train and landing on the *River Palace*, but I did wish to know about my brother's new life. It was hard to believe that a month had already slipped away. I was trying to imagine Zach's new home and school when Solomon's heavy boot landed on the roof.

"Come on, let's go see a friend of mine," Solomon said, shaking my knee. It sounded like a fine idea, seeing something besides cages to clean. "I just need you to help me with one chore first," Solomon said.

"All right," I answered. Some chores just couldn't be ignored, not even for one day.

"It's the elephant—"

"Ah, no, not elephants!" I interrupted. The elephant cages were the worst to clean up. I swear, it seemed like we were always dealing with one end or the other. They never could get enough to eat, and I never could shovel fast enough to keep their cage clean. People came to the circus to see the elephants more than anything else, but to me they meant only work. I was hoping to escape it for a day.

"It's not to shovel, Owen, you bellyacher." Solomon nudged me with his shoulder as we walked back down into the stable area.

"What for, then?" I asked.

"I need to put a salve on Tippo's feet and I want you to take Little Bet out of the cage while I do it."

"What's wrong with Tippo's feet?" I asked, relieved at the assignment.

"Hathaway is making her wire walk again. It's terrible on her feet. I need to shave her toenails and put a salve on the bottom."

I didn't often get to see the elephants in their cages. Their trainer, Mendeley, had them out walking around town with a banner to advertise the show, or learning new tricks or performing. Little Bet was nestled under her momma, trying to nurse. Tippo kept trying to push her off, but Little Bet was stubborn too. I slipped a rope around her neck with a slip knot and coaxed her out of the cage using the nuts Solomon gave me.

"Don't let her step on your feet. You'll have a useless foot to match that arm," Solomon said. I didn't know if he was trying to be funny or not, but I didn't think it was much of a joke. Besides, I could move my arm a bit now if I concentrated real hard, though my hand was still a useless slab of meat.

Little Bet stood about the same height as me, but each of her legs was thick, near as big around as my waist. I patted her hide and scratched behind her ears like I'd seen Solomon do to Tippo. She liked it, I think, for she wrapped her trunk around my neck. The wet tip of it tickled my ear and made me giggle.

"Now quit that!" I said to her and held out another nut. Like a finger, the tip of her trunk swiped the nut and then she popped it into her mouth. She seemed like she was smiling. Her eyes were bright and looked naughty somehow too. I could see the reflection of myself in her long-lashed amber eyes. As we walked by the horses, she started to unlatch the lock on the stall of Roman, the great white leading show horse.

"No! Little Bet, you can't let him out!" I pushed her surprisingly strong trunk away from the gate and picked up our pace. I headed for the circus ring, where she couldn't cause too much trouble. I walked her around a few times and imagined myself as her trainer. I only thought about what I'd announce to the audience since I promised Zach I'd never be a braggart anymore—

Ladies and gentlemen! Boys and girls! Direct your attention to the great Owen Burke, the world's greatest master of the world's greatest beasts! Elephants, lions, and bears bow to his commands!

"Up, Little Bet, up!" I said, pretending I was Mendeley. I raised my right arm above my head like I'd seen him do, though of course he could use both of his arms. Tippo would sit right back on her very large bottom and then lift her front feet into the air with that command. Little Bet, instead, reached down and explored my private parts.

"She's looking for a nut!" Solomon laughed, walking into the ring.

I was about to defend my honor, when I understood his comment. "Oh, you mean a nut in my pocket," I said, my face turning red. Solomon laughed the whole way back to the elephant cage, his shoulders twitching.

"Come on, now," he said, trying to pull himself together, "let's go see my friend while there's still light."

"You have a friend here?" I asked, changing the subject.

"Sure do," he said, giving me a broad smile.

"How do you even know where we are?" I'd stopped asking where we were after the second day because it didn't seem to matter any.

"Why, we're in Ripley, Ohio. My favorite spot on all the rivers," Solomon said, gesturing to the cluster of homes.

"Why's that? Looks like all the other towns, if you ask me."

"Well, it's not," he answered just as our feet hit land. I felt odd being on dry land again—a bit queasy, like I'd had too much gravy with my biscuits, which I had.

"What's so special about it?" I asked, trying to keep up with Solomon's long strides.

"It's the hurricane gonna blow through this country." His voice was more alive than I'd ever heard it sound, almost like a preacher's who'd had too much coffee before church.

"What do you mean, Solomon?" I asked, though I didn't want to hear a sermon. This was my day off.

He dropped his voice then and I had to nearly run to keep up with him so I could hear.

"This is the center of antislavery, Owen. Hundreds of people here in Ripley are working to change the laws." His voice changed from light to serious, and I almost regretted having changed the topic.

"What laws?"

"Proslavery ones," he answered. His face clouded up and he looked off into the distance like he was remembering something.

"You mean they're abolitionists?" I asked. I knew that word from the spinsters. They said Quakers hated slavery the way Baptists hated alcohol.

"Yes, exactly," he answered, obviously glad I had some knowledge of it all. It felt strange to be out here on this path with Solomon instead of our stall. He seemed more relaxed, friendlier. His shoulders looked softer and so did his eyes. We went along in silence for a spell—it was nice to hear something other than loud music and hooves. The sounds of birds overhead felt new, like they do in spring.

Wanting to please Solomon, all of a sudden I broke the silence. "I knew some spinsters who were abolitionists back in Pittsburgh."

Solomon stopped walking and stared right down into my face and asked real serious, "What did you think of it?"

The truth was I hadn't thought about it at all. I didn't read their newsletter even when I was folding it. Slavery just was. I hadn't questioned it any more than I'd questioned why leather was brown. What could I say? I'd be lying to say I was an abolitionist. I was nothing to nobody, really.

"I thought they printed a fine newsletter about it," I answered. "My brother, Zach, and I helped fold it." Just mentioning Zach's name aloud made my voice tear like paper.

"You're a fine boy, Owen. A fine boy." Solomon ruffled my hair and smiled. Of course, he didn't know I was a liar and the fine boy was Zachary, a boy he would never even meet.

CHAPTER

11

WE SPENT ALL AFTERNOON with John Parker's family, enjoying a home-cooked meal of chicken and dumplings and apple pie. I even got to play a ball game with their older son. Though it was a fine sunny afternoon, Solomon and John Parker stayed busy talking quietly in the barn. When we got back to the boat just a couple of hours later, several farmers stood around the front of the boat talking to Lord Hathaway. One of them had a lamb under one arm, another had a small calf on a leather strap, and yet another farmer had an old dog on a frayed rope. Solomon said, "Oh no," and stationed himself at the edge of the crowd to listen. I stuck by his side, of course.

"You've done tricked us, you no good slicker!" shouted the largest farmer, a stout man who held a small lamb under his arm and shook a handbill with the other.

"I have done no such thing. That handbill," Hathaway said, pointing to the crumpled paper in the man's hands, "says my lions need live meat—not that I would pay you for it." I noticed Hathaway stayed on the plank that made him seem nearly as tall as the farmers in front of him.

"Ridiculous! You expect us to hand over our livestock for free?" The man's voice was louder now, and thick with anger. His plump face was red as a tomato. Murmurs of approval rippled from the audience, and Solomon stiffened beside me.

The men in the crowd looked rough and a bit dangerous. I wouldn't want to make them mad.

"'Tis your choice." Hathaway coughed behind a spotless white-gloved hand, then continued. "But your chance of ever seeing such a spectacle again in your life is, well, slim."

His voice showed his contempt for the rough crowd beneath him. It was obvious that he thought much more of himself.

"We ought to get Sheriff Jones and tell him about your scam," the farmer threatened.

"Fetch him if you must," Hathaway answered, crossing his arms and shifting his weight as if bored, "but I suspect he'd prefer to see this spectacle than listen to your complaining."

The crowd was thicker now, with more men and even more animals. I tried to ask Solomon what was going on, but he hushed me.

"You can have this cur," a young man said, holding out the tattered rope to Lord Hathaway, "but she ain't none too fresh!" That made a ripple of laughter spread out across the crowd. Lord Hathaway didn't reach for the rope, but turned sideways and gestured to the man. "Come aboard, then, son. You can watch for free."

"Thank you," the farmer answered, and the dog trotted up behind him, her tail wagging.

"Anyone else?" Lord Hathaway asked.

"I'll carry her home for stew before turning her over to the likes of you," the stout farmer said, and stalked off past Solomon and me. Now I saw why he carried the lamb; her left paw looked broken.

"I can't just give up this calf," a different farmer said, in a voice like sandpaper.

"What if I offered you tickets for tomorrow's performance for your entire family?" Lord Hathaway said.

"It might tempt me."

"You can sit in the front row"—Hathaway smiled broadly—"and enjoy all our refreshments as a courtesy."

"Can I see the private show that night?" the farmer

asked, and for some reason red started crawling up his neck. I had no idea what show he meant. I did sometimes see men climb aboard the *Palace* late at night and head up to Hathaway's stateroom, but I always thought that was for poker. Maybe it was some type of special show. I'd have to ask Solomon about it later.

"You drive a hard bargain, but yes," Lord Hathaway answered, and the calf and the farmer waited in front of the main doors. Though the business had obviously been completed, Lord Hathaway just stood there, and silence hung in the air for just a moment.

One of the men in the back spoke up. He had his hat pulled down low over his eyes, and he looked like a towner, but I recognized him as a worker on the *Palace*.

"I'd like to see them lions take that meat," he said, loud enough for everyone to hear. Many men grunted and nodded their agreement. He was playing a shill, trying to get the crowd to do what Hathaway wanted by pretending he was one of them. I didn't know exactly what was unfolding, but it all felt dark and wrong somehow. Solomon's face was painted in a scowl, his eyebrows knit over his hooded eyes and his lips pressed tightly together.

"That could be arranged for a dime," Lord Hathaway announced.

"It's illegal to make money on the Lord's Day," a man midcrowd retorted.

"Hardly an inconvenience," Hathaway answered, having anticipated this objection. "Have you a nearby asylum? Or an orphanage, perhaps?"

"We got an orphanage," an elderly man answered.

"Well, I shall donate a nickel for every dime you offer. Does that satisfy you?"

Clearly it did. The men dug in their pockets and each produced a dime, or borrowed enough from a friend, dropping their coins into a grinder's hat and then following Hathaway onto the boat and through the theater. Below, in the circus ring, the lions' cage had already been pushed into the center.

The lions were agitated, having not been fed their regular ration. The men crowded into the ring rather than take a place in the fancy upholstered seats. Hathaway folded his arms and the lion trainer came around the giant cage. The trainer did not wear his flashy performance wardrobe and looked fairly like one of the farmers in his everyday britches and linen cloth shirt.

"My name is Paul O'Claire. I am the head animal trainer here on the *River Palace*. I see you have brought gifts for my lions."

The men murmured and talked amongst themselves. I finally understood what was about to happen. It made me feel both sick to my stomach and completely unable to tear my eyes away. O'Claire came first to get the small, elderly dog from the young man.

"Would you like to do the honors?"

"No, sir. This is as close as I ever plan to get to a lion." The man backed away with his palms in the air.

The dog was sniffing happily in the sawdust, finding bits of treats the trainers used to get the performing animals to do their tricks. The bottom of the cage was waist high to most of the men, so the little dog could never know what paced above her. Quick as a flash, O'Claire picked up the dog, trotted up the ramp, opened the cage door, and pitched her inside with the lions. The constant murmuring that had gone on since the farmers came aboard stopped. All eyes were riveted to the small black dog cowering in the corner of the cage.

Solomon tried to turn me away, but I resisted. He shook his head. All at once, the female lion pounced on the dog, which gave one sharp yelp and then was silent. The lioness clamped her powerful jaws into the neck and shook the dog once. There came a sound like a stick cracking underfoot and I knew the dog's neck had been broken. With one paw the lion held the dog's body in place. I slammed my eyes shut, but I could still hear the terrible sound of the lion's jaws working over the dog. The male lion paced behind her and roared so loud it seemed to rattle my own bones. I looked to see the lioness drop the dog, letting Lalla Rookh, the male, have the carcass.

"Who's next?" O'Claire asked the crowd, who were still silently watching the lions.

"I'll go," said the man with the calf, "but I'd like to deliver the meat myself."

My stomach dropped to my knees and a bitter taste filled my mouth. It wasn't meat he had on a rope, least not yet. It was a calf still wobbly on her feet. O'Claire stepped aside and the farmer struggled to push the calf up the ramp to the cage door. O'Claire followed him and instructed him to shove the calf's hind end into the cage as soon as he pulled back the door. I decided I'd seen enough blood for one day, so I asked Solomon if I could go clean a cage or mop the deck. Anything but this. Solomon nodded his approval.

Just as I started to turn from the grisly scene, Paul O'Claire yelled, "Oh, NO!"

The calf slipped off the ramp and onto the sawdust below, while the farmer fell to his knees, his shoulders, arm, and head now in the opening of the cage door.

What happened next seemed to move like it was in a nightmare. As the lion rushed the door, O'Claire tried to slam the gate, but the poor farmer was still wedged in the way. The twenty or so men scrambled in every direction, yelling and cursing like pirates. A few rushed up the ramp to help pull their neighbor out of harm's way, while others made for the steps and out to dry land.

As I watched in horror, the lion slashed his mighty paw across the farmer's back and arm, shredding the man's shirt and flesh. His scream was the worst sound I ever heard. Solomon pushed the frantic men out of his way, grabbed the farmer's legs, and pulled him from the opening of the cage and into the ring.

The lion surged again for the opening while O'Claire and a negro struggled to hold the gate shut. The lion slowly pulled back into the cage, but its paw kept swiping around the bars, as if looking for more flesh.

Seeing that the lion was now mostly contained, a few of the men who had stood by dazed and stupefied, like me, now sprung into action and rushed up the ramp to help.

The men pushed harder than they probably needed now, since only the lion's paw still stuck out of the cage. Its terrible roar filled the whole hippodrome.

"Stop!" O'Claire yelled at the top of his voice.

The men stopped pushing. The ring went silent. The lion pulled its paw back inside to safety, but it was obviously injured. He held it aloft and it dangled there, like a limb cracked by lightning. The farmer's face was the slate gray of fog, and the sawdust beneath him was smeared with bright blood. It was a god-awful mess and right or not, all the blame burned in the pit of my stomach for Lord Hathaway. Sure enough, Hathaway made us shove off from that town before nightfall, fearing an angry crowd looking for revenge. This was a part of the circus nobody wanted to see or think about when they're eating fancy nuts and laughing over a clown. Hell, I wished I hadn't seen it neither. Wish I could wipe it clean out of my mind.

CHAPTER

12

"NO! ZACH, NO!"

"Owen." Solomon's voice found me. "Owen, wake up now." His strong hands grabbed my shoulders and rattled me to my senses. I was dreaming a lion was eating Zach. Ever since that night with the farmers, I'd been dreaming about that lion getting loose. It was the first time I'd seen Zach in a dream though, and that haunted me more than the lions did.

"Let's get some breakfast," Solomon offered. "The *Attaboy* needs a heavy cleaning."

I pulled on my britches, which were getting too snug around the waist with all the food I'd been eating. "What will we do over there?" I asked.

"More cleaning, 'course," Solomon answered. "I'm surprised you got to ask what we're doing by now."

It was true. We cleaned something most hours of every day. We didn't spend as much time on the *Attaboy*, and I was looking forward to a change. Amazing how fast even the circus could feel ordinary.

Most of the performers slept on the *Attaboy*. Hathaway stayed on the *Palace* in a grand suite near the front, but all the performers and their families had miniature homes aboard the steamer.

Solomon had me waxing the wood paneling that surrounded the small amphitheater on the *Attaboy*. It was sticky and grimy from people's hands smearing the wood on their way through. Down on the stage, the freaks were taking their midday meal. It was the only place large enough to serve them on the *Attaboy*, I guess since so many of the freaks needed help getting their food, or maybe 'cause they couldn't walk much they were served their meals here instead of on the *Palace*. And waiters fetched whatever the freaks asked for, like in a real fancy restaurant.

Only a few of the freaks were ever brought to the *Palace* to make brief appearances during the show. This little bit teased patrons into paying an extra dime to visit the *Attaboy* after the big show. For that dime people could stare at the freaks all they wanted and listen to a minstrel band. Most folks coughed up the extra coin when they got a gander at the two-headed woman. I was aching to get a closer look myself.

We had your regular freaks on the *River Palace*— your fat lady, a living skeleton, a bearded woman, an armless painter, a dwarf couple who they called Mr. and Mrs. Thimble (though they weren't married). Lord Hathaway tried to make some of them seem even more grand, giving them fancy names—the American Obelisk (he must've been near to eight feet), the Colossal Cowgirl (she was just a bit shorter than the Obelisk), and the Last of the Lost Tribe of Xanadu (he was just an Indian they dressed up all fancy and painted his face).

I tried to keep my mind on my work, but I knew Hathaway wasn't on the *Attaboy* and Solomon was up on deck. I was itching to see how much the fat lady really ate and how the armless man got the food up to his mouth and whether the dwarfs used high chairs like some people said they did. I shouldn't have left my job just to spy, but after two months on the *Palace*, I hadn't swallowed all my curiosities just yet. I pretended like I needed to clean the chairs on the lowest level next to the stage so I could get me an eyeful.

The armless man sat right next to the fat lady, who had pushed together two chairs to hold her wideness.

The armless man had his feet up on the table and a fork was wedged between his toes. He wiped his chin with a napkin that was held by the toes on his other foot. It almost seemed normal. The dwarfs weren't sitting by each other and they did not have high chairs. They sat on wood boxes that were placed on regular old chairs. The living skeleton didn't have much on his plate, to be sure. But he didn't look all that different from most of the kids at the orphanage, with those sunken eyes and hollow cheeks.

Our best freaks, the ones that pulled in the most money, were Molly-Catherine. They were twins born stuck together at the backbone. I knew enough about babies to know it was a miracle they and their momma ever survived the birth, especially since they were born as slaves on a North Carolina plantation. Their momma wanted them, strange as they were, which is more than I can say for my own momma. Solomon had told me about them one night before we fell asleep.

He said they'd been rented out to scalawags who put them on exhibition (sometimes without benefit of clothes) just to make their master rich. He said they'd traveled all the way to England, even had tea with the queen herself! I wondered how they'd managed to buy their freedom, but they must have somehow because they dressed in the finest clothes and wore ropes of jewelry. Hathaway must have a soft place for them or maybe they were good negotiators on top of everything else. The young women sat at the head of the freak table and each head talked to the person sitting on her side. Truth was that it looked like identical twins were just sharing a chair.

When they performed they wore an outfit that was just one wide dress, but now they had on two different dresses. Only their shoes matched.

Molly said to the Skeleton Man, *"C'est une fourchette. Dire 'a fourchette.'"*

The Skeleton Man tried to repeat the sounds and the smooth way they spilled off her tongue, but his strange accent got in the way and it sounded like he was gargling.

"Lovely!" Molly said. "Lovely first attempt, Daniel."

Strange, I know, but hearing the Skeleton Man's real name felt like a kick to the gut. I never thought of the freaks being like regular folks with Christian names. Of course, his momma didn't name him the Skeleton Man neither. I wonder what she thought about him earning a living being on some sideshow. Sure he probably made more money than was possible doing most regular jobs, but did it shame her? Would it shame my own momma to know I was nothing but a circus grunt who shoveled animal dirt?

I wiped off the arms of the cane chairs with a sudsy rag, trying to get the stickiness off. I focused on the front rows so I could still hear them talking to each other.

Molly and the fat lady were having a lively discussion about their recent purchases.

"If you didn't spend so much on shoes, dear Nellie, you could have fancier dresses!" Molly advised the fat lady.

"But you know my weakness for pretty shoes, Molly, and it's not like you can pass by a hat without purchasing it either!" the fat lady teased.

"True enough!" Molly answered. "I believe a hat is the crown to any ensemble."

"Is that the excuse you're using this week?" Nellie answered with a wink.

Molly reached over and swatted her hand for teasing her, and they both broke into giggles. They sounded like friends who grew up together.

They continued their friendly banter, finishing their fried chicken in delicate bites. I expected the fat woman to stuff her face with the offerings, but she set her fork down between each bite just like the slender Molly-Catherine.

As I moved down the row, a discussion between the armless man and the Colossal Cowgirl kept getting louder and more intense.

"I don't believe in long-term investments like land and houses," the armless man said, a bit louder than necessary it seemed to me since the cowgirl was sitting right next to him.

"Well," she answered in an even tone, "that's your prerogative, of course, but I consider it foolish." She swiped the last sliver of strawberry pie off her dessert plate and ate it.

"Don't call me foolish!" The armless man dropped the heel of his foot on the table and made the silverware jump. The whole table went quiet and everyone looked down at the two of them.

"Now, Paul"—the American Obelisk leaned toward the armless man—"Jenny means well, you know that. She just wants you to think about your future is all."

"It's true," Jenny answered. "I just don't want to see you end up in a hospital or a home."

The armless man, I mean, Paul, nodded slightly.

"I 'spect you're right about that part, anyway," he answered finally. Everyone at the table nodded their approval and went back to their own conversations and plates. Then Paul cut a piece of chicken breast and smeared it into the brown gravy on his plate. For a moment I forgot that he was using his feet instead of hands to eat. Jenny put her arm around his shoulders then and gave him a little squeeze. He blushed a bit under her touch. My own face got hot realizing that I'd been staring and not even working for a spell. I went to get fresh water and soap to finish my work. I could no longer hear their conversations but that felt right somehow. They sounded like a real family, I guess, getting into squabbles, teasing each other, and sharing meals. Maybe they were even better, somehow, than my own family 'cause at least they were together. My family was a pile of rags now—shredded and torn.

CHAPTER

"What on God's green planet is that?" I asked Solomon, sitting up in my straw bed to an ear-splitting sound that filled the ship.

It was early in the morning, too early to be hearing something that awful. I wondered if Little Bet or Tippo or one of the other beasts was dying.

"I'm sure I don't know," answered Solomon. We followed the sound out of the stable area, through the ring, and up the carpeted steps out onto the main deck. Apparently, so had everyone else. A giant set of pipes had been lugged on board. A worker I recognized from the stables cranked a handle on the side of a large metal contraption and a musician plucked at a small keyboard. Little mouths on the top of large pipes opened and closed, creating loud notes that sounded something like "My Old Kentucky Home," but with a headache.

Lord Hathaway was obviously real proud of this new addition to his circus. He put on his performance voice though there weren't any rubes, or customers, around to hear him. I found myself standing next to a boy with a shock of red hair. He seemed to be about the same age as Zach, and I was surprised I hadn't noticed him on board before. 'Course he was probably in a performance family anyway, and they did not mix with the working hands. Shoot, they were like royalty compared to us. We ranked lower than the animals we served. But I missed the company of other boys. I was tired of pretending to be a man.

"This calliope is the grandest invention for the circus in the last thirty years, perhaps of all time! Now folks will hear this circus coming from miles away!"

"Too bad it might make them want to run miles away," I whispered to the redhead. He laughed loud, which got him a dirty look from Lord Hathaway.

Lord Hathaway continued with his tirade, not just of details about the calliope, but also about how the *Palace* needed to have better ticket sales. While he went on and on, I leaned over to talk to the boy.

"I'm Owen."

"Caleb."

"What's your job?"

"Printer. Well, it's my dad's job, but I help. My mom and sister are in the show." His voice had a slight accent to it, but I couldn't quite place it. I'd never heard anything like it before.

"What act?"

"Equestrians."

"You don't take to the saddle yourself?" In most circus families, everybody performed.

"Too clumsy. What about you?"

"I work with the hay burners." It wasn't quite a lie. I didn't much work with the animals, only what they left behind.

"Is your dad the Lion King?" Caleb asked, obviously impressed. I almost answered yes. It had been so long since I'd impressed anybody.

"Nah." I stared at the tips of my boots. Parentage was not a topic I wanted to stay on.

"Come down to the press room sometime. I'll show you how it works. Maybe I can come see the animals get fed. I heard about that man almost getting his head tore off by Lalla Rookh."

Obviously he'd gotten the grander version of the events. Embellishment ruled the circus.

"I saw it happen," I bragged, and then immediately felt bad for trying to impress him with the bloody scene that still haunted my nights.

"You did not!" he challenged, obviously impressed. "Tell me the whole story!"

I missed bragging to a set of willing ears. So I started, "First, a group of farmers were tricked into—"

"Ahem," Lord Hathaway interrupted us. All eyes were on us. Silence fell as heavy as an elephant.

"Am I interrupting your discourse?" Lord Hathaway asked, his voice mocking.

"No, sir," we both said simultaneously.

"Are you quite sure? Because I could instruct my staff at a more convenient hour and locale if it would please you." His voice did not disguise his disgust.

"No, sir," we both answered again.

"Shut your hole, Caleb," a large man said, leaning down into the boy's ear. His hair was also aflame, so I figured it must be Caleb's father.

"Well, then, as I was saying," Lord Hathaway began again, "tonight we cross the Mason-Dixon Line. The flags, the music, the jokes all must be considered to please our Southern brethren." I thought he was done and I started to turn away, but he cleared his throat and then continued.

"Oh, yes, I nearly forgot. I will no longer be needing the services of the brass ensemble. The calliope has replaced you handily. Please pack your things and disembark."

I felt sorry for the three band members, who suddenly found themselves unemployed. I would miss the joyful sounds of their parade before shows, which always led townspeople to the boat. It was wildly unfair, as usual for Hathaway. The crowd must have agreed because grumbles rippled out over the performers and workers gathered on the deck.

"Wrathy me not!" he yelled, "or you shall join them on the banks of this mighty river!"

The crowd silenced. He clapped his hands twice, replaced his ridiculously tall stovepipe hat, and dismissed us.

I started following Solomon off the deck and back down into the stables. We weren't three steps down before Solomon started reprimanding me for talking in front of Lord Hathaway.

"You were spared because that boy's momma is a headliner and his daddy the advance man," Solomon said shortly. His shoulder knocked me soundly as we descended the steps. He had no patience for me, I could tell.

I didn't know what an advance man did, but I figured it must be important.

"You know what Hathaway's capable of," he reminded me. I shivered just to think of my dip in the Allegheny River.

Just as we hit the bottom step, Caleb's father stopped us. His red hair shone like fire in the bright sunlight.

"Solomon!" he called. Solomon stopped and I did too, a bit afraid of the booming voice that followed us. We waited for him to catch up.

"Solomon, who is this boy?"

"This is Owen Burke, sir." Solomon always looked at his feet when he answered white men, and this time was no different.

"But who is he, Solomon? Who does he belong to?" He punctuated every word, like Solomon was too stupid to understand the language he was using.

"He belongs to me," Solomon answered quickly, obviously trying to end this line of questioning as soon as he could. Caleb's father sucked in his breath and then crossed him arms in front of his chest. He glowered down at Solomon.

"No white boy belongs to a Negro slave." He hissed the words and then spit a wad of tobacco at Solomon's feet. I would have to scrub that spot later, I knew. It made me dislike this man. I was dying to correct him and say that Solomon wasn't anyone's slave, but I didn't dare. You could tell he wasn't a man often crossed.

"I mean, sir, he belongs with me, not to me," Solomon answered quietly, dropping his eyes again. I hated to see him cower to these men.

Caleb's dad turned to me then, and lifted my chin and looked in my eyes. He inspected my hair, which was odd, but I realized he was looking for fleas and lice. Living with the animals had made them near impossible to keep off, especially in my hay bed.

"Where are your parents, son?"

"Dead," I answered. "Dead to me." I didn't like the way he had talked to Solomon, so I didn't care what he thought of me. I didn't like his inspection of me either, like I was a piece of beef he was deciding on for his dinner table. He even grabbed my right hand and inspected my fingers. I wondered what he would think of my lame arm, but I didn't bring it to his attention.

"Small fingers. Good for press work," he stated. "You had any schooling?"

"I read and write some. Not much for numbers."

"Owen, you are to report to me every day after breakfast. When you're done setting the type, then the animals"—he paused to stare at Solomon like a dare—"can have you back."

Solomon dropped his head.

"But Solomon needs my help." It was as far as I could go to disagree with him. It felt puny. I felt puny.

"Anybody can muck a stall, boy—but not anybody can set type. Report tomorrow morning after breakfast."

"Tomorrow?" I asked again, surprised how fast everything had changed.

"Tomorrow!" he answered, "and leave your attitude with the animals!"

"Yes, sir," I answered. If he was going to be my new boss, I'd be a fool to start out on the wrong step with him.

Solomon and I walked back to our stall in silence. I realized how I'd gotten used to Solomon's permanent presence in my days. He was like the tree in the courtyard of the orphanage. I didn't really think about him, but I was always glad enough to see him. Solomon's shoulders were slumped and his lips were turned down in a frown. I wanted to clap him on the back and tell him it would be fine, but we did not make such gestures toward each other. Even my good hand felt useless at my side.

Solomon slid open our stall. The early-morning light spilled onto my wool blanket. Tacked above my pallet was a handbill of the show I'd found under a seat, and its big letters and pictures were the only fancy thing in the room. Still, this small corner felt safe and good, like vegetable soup on a rainy day. It was the most humble of places, but it had, in these few short weeks, become home.

CHAPTER 14

THAT NIGHT WAS THE BEST I'd had on the ship since the first time Solomon snuck me on board. Perhaps it was because of Caleb's father, but Solomon helped me shovel out the animal cages double time and then he and I snuck up into the secret spot where he'd first hidden me. It seemed much smaller with him wedged under there with me, but it was more fun to share it with someone. Together we watched the circus from beginning to end.

A man drove forty horses around the ring! The reins stretched over the rows and rows of the all-white horses. Not once did he lose his balance standing on the back of two mares in the last row. More equestrians followed, each trick more daring than the last. I thought the pantomine was an odd thing to behold, and the posture masters were like tangled up bits of flesh. My favorite acts were with the animals. I had thought that Zelda's bear act couldn't be topped, but I had never gotten to see the Lion King himself in the ring before. Cracking his whip, he made those cats leap from one pedestal to another and even through rings ablaze with fire. One cat was still missing, Lalla Rookh, because her paw hadn't healed yet. As thrilling as it was to see the lions, I couldn't wait to see Tippo and Little Bet.

Tippo was led out by Mendeley. A woman in a fancy costume with lots of sparkles led Little Bet around the hippodrome so the audience could see her. Little Bet moved haphazardly along the path, throwing her trunk around like she wasn't sure how to control it. And she ran for a few paces and then walked extra slow, giving the woman trying to control her a difficult time of it. She was only able to get her back in line with the nuts. Finally, Little Bet stood still (well, almost anyway) and watched her momma's performance. Solomon told me it was so she could learn from watching and get accustomed to the applause and cheers of the audience.

Tippo did a series of tricks—standing on her head, rolling a ball around the ring while she was balanced on her back feet, sitting back and begging for a treat. At last she was brought up four large steps and then she walked across a wire to a set of other steps. The wire stretched just over the top of Mendeley's head and was only an elephant's-length long. Still, it was amazing to watch that giant beast walk across the rope. Not once did she teeter or sway. Confident and graceful as a cat. As she walked down the steps, I exhaled slowly. I hadn't realized I'd been holding my breath for her.

"Don't you never mistreat an elephant," Solomon said as Tippo took an ovation. The crowd thundered their approval of Tippo and her calf.

"Why's that?" I asked, curious, though I can't imagine having the nerve to hurt something so big.

"'Cause they never forget a cruel trainer. They'll get you back first chance they get," he answered, looking right at me. He seemed suddenly disinterested in the show, which now had a dozen white horses filing into the ring.

"That so?" I said, disbelieving. An elephant could be trained to walk a tightrope, but hold a grudge just like a person? I doubted it.

"Don't believe me if you don't want. But don't you never mistreat an elephant either." He looked down as the equestrian director climbed onto the back of the last row of horses and began to urge them around the ring, faster and faster. But it didn't seem all that impressive after Tippo's performance. We were quiet for a few minutes, just watching the horses.

"Mendeley smacks Tippo every day," I said, wincing at the thought of him cracking the gold tip of his cane across her trunk to get her into line.

"I know," Solomon answered, and his eyes got wide and he raised his eyebrows too.

I thought Solomon was being a bit superstitious. How else would a man get a giant animal to do what he said? Besides, the animal trainers were always bragging about God giving them dominion over the animal kingdom.

Hercules Libby came out after that and impressed everyone by plucking women from the audience to lift in their cane-bottom chairs. Solomon told me all the women actually worked for the circus and were skinny as eight-year-old girls, only padded to look like heavy matrons. The women knew how to sit still and not shift their weight on Hercules.

The last act had the Siamese twins, Molly-Catherine, come out just a bit to wave to the audience and then shuffle back behind the heavy velvet curtain, to tease the folks into visiting the *Attaboy*.

For the grand finale, Mademoiselle Marie walked a wire from the ring to the ceiling of the *Palace*, pushing a wheelbarrow the whole time. Beneath, all the clowns and posture masters crowded into the ring or around the hippodrome. Hercules and all the other acts came out at once to astound the audience. My eyes felt like they would burst with so much to see! My chest felt swollen, too, knowing that I was a part of all this now, even if it was a part no audience would ever see. It made me proud and happy. I started to think about how much Zach would love to be here beside me too, but I pushed down thoughts of my brother so that I could hold this moment and remember it always. I wished I had one of them fancy daguerreotype contraptions so I could always look at the image of this wonderful chaos. When the whole audience was on their feet clapping louder than a thunderstorm, Lord Hathaway came out and took a bow like he himself was the best performer of all.

Solomon and I stayed up late into the night, talking about all we had seen. It was the best day ever on the *River Palace*. The best day of my whole life so far.

CHAPTER

THE NEXT MORNING, just after dawn, Solomon walked me to the print room.

"You mind Mr. Greene now," he warned me.

"I will," I answered, worried as to what I might end up doing with my days. I felt almost like a schoolboy getting dropped off by his pa.

"See you at supper," Solomon said, then walked away without turning back.

Inside the room was an enormous machine that filled about half the space. It was nearly as large as a wagon. Two large Negroes operated the monstrosity. Their work seemed almost like a dance, the way they moved so rhythmically—adding paper and rolling it in, pressing down to make an imprint, rolling it back out, and then plucking it to hang like laundry on strings that stretched across the room.

Caleb stood on a wood box in front of a giant podium. In his left hand he held something wooden, and he kept plucking little pieces of metal and sorting it. Caleb's dad finally saw me standing in the doorway, a bit dazed by all the movement and motion of the press and its workers.

"Come in, Owen," Mr. Greene ordered. I followed him, careful where I stepped around the stacks of handbills and posters on the floor.

"This is our press," he explained. "We print every sheet that gets tacked to barns and inside shop windows for the *Palace*." I didn't know what to say, so I didn't say anything. I just nodded.

"We even print the booklets about the freaks to sell as the rubes leave the boat. Those pamphlets pay for the rest of the work we do here." I was trying to follow along with what he was talking about, but I had never seen one of the pamphlets.

"Caleb will teach you how to set the type," he said leading me over to the boy's side.

Now he turned his attention to his son.

"Caleb, we got to get these rags posted over Dan Rice's in Cincinnati. So don't dawdle." Then he left in a hurry.

"Hi, Owen," Caleb said with a smile so wide his gums showed.

"Caleb, you going to show me what to do?" I asked, though I knew the answer.

"It's not hard." He nodded to another wooden frame, shaped like a paddle with rows in it. I grabbed it with my right hand and put it in my left. I squeezed the handle the best I could. Caleb caught himself staring and then asked, "What's the matter?"

"I need some help to hold this durn thing. Do you have a rag?" I asked.

"Sure. What for?"

"So's I can tie this paddle to my left hand. It's what I do downstairs when I'm working." He jumped off the box and headed for a basket in the corner. It was an inky rag that he tore, but he helped me tie the galley to my hand. He showed me how to find the letters and pictures and put them into the right places.

"We're lucky," he said after a few minutes of quiet. Just the pounding of the press behind us, with the two workers in constant motion.

"Why's that?" I remembered to answer after a moment—I was concentrating so hard on the tiny letters, it was hard to do anything else.

" 'Cause we only have to do the typesetting for these circus sheets. Some of these letters are giant and take up so much space. Can you imagine doing this for a whole newspaper?" I could not. It would take forever to turn out a whole newspaper.

We worked silently for a while. Normally I'd try to fill up that space with talking, but my brain almost burned with this very different work. Why, I hadn't seen words except circus posters since that day at the spinster sisters' house. I thought back to that day with Zachary and the cinnamon cookies. I could almost smell them and see his little face so serious, studying the paper. It seemed so long ago. I slowed down by daydreaming, and Caleb nudged me with his elbow.

"Tell me about working with the animals," Caleb begged.

"It ain't much, not really," I answered, not wanting to go into details about waxing, scrubbing, and shoveling animal dirt.

"Do you help train them?" he asked, his voice full of admiration and wonder.

It wouldn't have been that long ago that I'd have taken this chance to tell a whole story with such a willing audience. I would make myself important and the star of the show, too. But it felt wrong now.

"Naw," I admitted to him, "I mostly just clean."

"Huh. Well, at least you get to see all them wild animals anytime you want."

"That's true," I agreed. Even if the work was messy, it was something to look at those big beasts. 'Course by now they seemed like almost any other kind of stock. Just a big cow or a large horse. We settled into work then, and the time went faster when I thought about the words used to describe the acts.

HERCULES LIBBY, the most POWERFUL man ALIVE! who has just returned from a protracted tour throughout Europe, and who, in all the capitals of the Old World, as well as throughout the length and breadth of North America is universally acknowledged as the strongest, most astonishing specimen of male strength.

✦　✦　✦

MAD'LLE LAKE, the astonishing WIRE WALKER, will walk a SINGLE WIRE 200 FEET in length from the dress circle to the FLAG!

✦　✦　✦

PROF. MENDELEY will showcase his splendid ELE-PHANT, TIPPO SULTAN, with a special appearance of her baby elephant, LITTLE BET.

✦　✦　✦

World-renowned EQUESTRIAN Mrs. LAKE and her daughter, the lovely and talented GWENDOLYN, in celebrated scenes of equitation and athletic feats.

I was just getting ready to ask Caleb if that was his ma and sister when he asked, "You hungry?"

"I can always eat!" I answered. I had gained considerable pounds since boarding the *Palace* and my britches squeezed me around the middle something awful. They were way above my ankles too, but it kept them out of the animal muck, so I didn't care.

I followed Caleb down off the boat along the bank and on board the *Attaboy*. Caleb ran the steps two at a time and then dodged around the balcony to a stateroom door. Inside was a living area that I could never describe, even using the most wonderous of words. There was a purple velvet settee and two chairs that looked like they'd been stuffed with hundreds of duck feathers. A glass-topped table held fresh flowers, a set of fancy teacups, and a bright silver-colored pot that I could see my ragged reflection in upside down. Real oil paintings of a woman and a beautiful girl on a horse were above a painted table. This was a far cry from my animal stall in the bowels of the *Palace*. I stood glued to the spot in the center of the floor like the fancy statue sitting next to the fresh flowers. I'd read about rich people before, but I hadn't never seen it firsthand. It even smelled rich—like biscuits and flowers. I felt like the messes I cleaned up. Like I didn't belong. While I stood there Caleb busted through a swinging door into another small room and started opening and shutting drawers and cabinets with loud thuds. I followed him into a small kitchen area that had painted cabinets and pulls that looked like jewelry. He yanked out a loaf of bread and a glass jar of fruit preserves. He cut a large slab of bread for me and slathered it with the strawberry mixture.

He motioned for us to sit at a small counter. Just as I shoved a much-too-large piece in my mouth (the orphanage conduct still ruled my table manners—he who eats the fastest gets the mostest), that beautiful girl from the painting walked into the room. She was wearing fancy riding attire with a ruffled blouse and long sleeves. Her jacket was cut like a man's tuxedo, but it had been embroidered with sequins and intricate flowers. She had curly brown hair that framed her face and the same startling green eyes of her brother. I nearly gagged on my bread.

"Caleb, be quiet! Mother is resting," the girl said.

"I forgot."

"Well, show some consideration. And some manners. Introduce me to your friend." She smiled at me then and the whole world melted away behind her.

"This is Owen Burke. Father got him transferred into the print room to help me set type," he answered, his mouth still plenty full of preserves.

"Hello, Owen Burke," she said, and offered me her gloved hand. I wasn't sure whether I was supposed to kiss it or shake it or what, so I held it between us like a small white dove. "I am Gwendolyn Greene," she said, glaring at Caleb, who continued to stuff bread and jam into his face. "Perhaps you will have better luck teaching him manners?" She tilted her head toward her brother.

"I, uh . . . don't, uh, know" was all I could manage. I felt like a complete idiot. I would teach Caleb manners? He obviously came from a different world than me. Gwendolyn smiled again and then turned and left the room. You could tell she was used to having people stare at her. Whether it was from being a performer in the circus or just 'cause she was so beautiful, I didn't know. I stared at the swinging doors, hoping she would come back through them. Caleb interrupted my wishes.

"We best get back to work now," Caleb said, and he shot out of the room at the same pace that brought us here. We worked the rest of the morning and exchanged bits of our stories. I told him I was an orphan who had run away and ended up on the *Palace.* He told me that his family had come over from Ireland to be a part of this circus. That explained the accent I sometimes heard flit through Caleb's words, but was stronger in his father's. He'd had another sister, but she'd died on the passage over, and his momma just wasn't the same anymore. The only time his ma smiled now was when she was paid to—performing as an equestrian in the circus. I was surprised at how open he was, telling me about his sister (Bridget was her name) and his ma. But when I tried to say something about Zach and even about my own ma, the words snagged in my throat.

❖ ❖ ❖

We finished working just before suppertime, and I headed back down toward the stables and my other, dirtier, life. I was tired in a whole new way. My body didn't ache except for my hand, from trying to grip that paddle, and my arms and back weren't sore, but my head felt kind of dizzy after concentrating for so long. My eyes felt dry and stung. I wasn't that hungry, either—I thought I might ask Solomon to snatch me a biscuit for dinner, and I could rest before evening chores started.

"Oh, good," Solomon said. "You're back in time to help me."

I tried not to groan. "What do you need?" I asked, though I didn't really want to be helpful, not really.

"I need you to take Little Bet out of the cage again.

That giant pest won't let me work on her momma at all."

I smiled. This I didn't mind. Little Bet might be naughty, but she was like being with a kid again.

"Sure, Solomon."

◆ ◆ ◆

Little Bet was feeling more ornery than usual. It took a whole handful of nuts just to get her out of the cage. Then she flipped over a wooden sandwich board someone had just painted and it landed in straw and filth. When someone came back to put that on and head out into town to advertise the circus, they'd be real sore. I moved her away from the spot before it was discovered that I'd let it happen.

As we walked toward the ring, she pushed me up against a cage and held me there with her trunk. It felt like a tree grew up right out of the boat. I couldn't move nor hardly breathe for a second. Then she lifted her trunk and trumpeted loudly like she was just playing with me after all.

She picked up a hammer and started waving it around, and I was afraid she might bash my head in without even meaning to. Every time I reached for it, she pulled it away and held it over my head. I pretended to be interested in the white stallion, Roman, and she dropped the hammer to the ground. I didn't reach for it 'cause I knew she'd beat me to it. Instead I just walked faster to get her away from it.

When we ran into a large water barrel, she immediately started slurping up the water with her trunk. I thought elephants just drank straight through their trunk, but they don't. She'd siphon it up in there and then pour it into her mouth. It was not a very neat operation. She sprayed me with the fifth trunkful.

"Ahhh, Little Bet!" I said, laughing. It felt good to be wet and cooled down even if it was with water that an elephant spit up on me. She had drained the last of the barrel and was now looking for something else to get into.

A candy butcher, who sold mostly nuts, Mr. John, rounded the corner to see Little Bet kick over the barrel.

"God blest it all!" he said, marching up to us. "Did you let her drink that whole barrel?"

"Yes. I'm just trying—" I was going to say how I was watching her for Solomon, but he interrupted me.

"Don't you know better than that?" His hands were on his hips, just like my ma used to do.

"Better than what?" I asked

"You take bulls to the river to drink!" he yelled, stepping a bit too close to my face.

"I know," I said, because I did. Bulls drank from the river. You'd spend your whole day trying to fetch enough water to satisfy an elephant's thirst.

"Wasting rain water on a rubber cow! Now what am I going to make the lemonade out of?"

Solomon appeared and asked what happened. You could tell the candy butcher liked Solomon, because he calmed down a bit in his presence.

"Little Bet did it," he said, and nearly growled. "Drank every bit of fresh water out of the barrel."

"They do seem to like the rainwater best." Solomon winked at me but not so Mr. John could see him.

Strange that life on a river caused issues with water, but it sure did. Nobody drank out of the rivers. We dumped animal dirt in it by the barrowful, and we saw lots along the banks that could turn your stomach besides. My first chore every morning was to haul fresh drinking water from town if we hadn't had any rain. So I could see why the candy butcher was upset. It takes a whole lot of fresh water to make the lemonade.

"You could use the river water, I suppose," said Solomon, trying to be helpful.

"Nah. It'd taste like fish, or worse," he said, motioning to a wheelbarrow that had yet to be dumped.

"Here's something," I said, and went over by the supply closet. Outside it was a large water barrel.

Though it was full near to the brim, a pair of red stockings was floating on top. Solomon pulled them out, wrung them in his calloused dark hands, and hung them over a nearby clothesline. It made me wonder what Solomon could know about women's clothes: it felt odd somehow.

"Why, it's pink as a newborn pup's nose!" John said after he dipped a large glass pitcher into the barrel.

"Looks kind of fancy," I offered.

"That it does!" John smiled broadly, and clapped me on the back. His whole personality seemed to change then.

Later I saw all the patrons drinking the new fancy pink lemonade. It was touted as a circus specialty, and the *River Palace* became known for it. I don't know how they kept making it, but I ain't never had a cup of it since.

CHAPTER 16

IN THE DAYS THAT FOLLOWED, I became used to my new routine. Mornings I would report to the print room to work beside Caleb. Thankfully Mr. Greene himself was rarely there. Caleb told me that his dad often went ahead of the *Palace* with the advance team on a small steamer called the *Hummingbird* to stir up excitement and get folks ready to spend their coins when the *Palace* appeared a few days later.

Each day I stayed a bit longer with Caleb—eating lunch together, visiting his stateroom, any old excuse. As we moved south along the river, the heat was almost unbearable down in the stables, and the stench of all that different manure was something to avoid as long as possible.

"Come on, let's fish off the back of the *Attaboy* for a spell," Caleb said.

"I ought to get back down to the stables." I didn't think I'd be able to make up a good excuse for fishing, though I longed to figure one worthy. Maybe if I brought back a fresh carp for dinner, but of course we had no need for carp or any other of food. I turned to go.

Caleb grabbed my shoulder. "You'll be working until after supper. You ought to have some time off," Caleb said. He was right, but it didn't seem to matter. I'd be working until time for my bedroll in the hay. It was a long day that repeated itself six days out of seven. And even on the seventh, the elephant cage had to be cleaned. It couldn't be avoided for a whole day or it would fill up.

"Just for a spell. Then I've got to earn my keep," I said, thinking this was a fine compromise.

We went around the back of the *Attaboy* and cast our lines out into the muddy water, our legs dangling off the side and my pale feet like two fish under the cool, lapping waves. We didn't have to talk all the time now and that was easier. Easier to pretend Caleb was Zach sitting beside me. Easier not having to explain what happened to my parents.

When Mr. Greene showed up I thought I would be in serious trouble for not having reported back to

Solomon as soon as lunch was over. Instead, he smiled at Caleb and sat down next to him.

"Any luck?" he asked us.

"Nope, Pa," Caleb answered, "but it sure does feel good to put my dogs in the water."

"I guess I ought to be getting back down to the stables," I said, standing up and trying to stuff my feet back into the boots that had become much too tight almost overnight.

"Can't Owen stay for supper, Pa? He don't get enough to eat and all he ever does is work."

"He doesn't look like he's missed many meals," Mr. Greene answered, but he smiled at me when he said it.

"Please, Father? He's the only other boy aboard the whole *Palace*!"

"I can't anyway," I said to Caleb. "I've got to help get the cages cleaned out during the two o'clock show."

Nothing surprised me more than when Mr. Greene shook his head and said, "Solomon can handle it. And you could use a decent bath. I'll go tell him not to expect you until the seven o'clock."

"Thank you, Mr. Greene. I really appreciate it." And I did, too, but I felt a little guilty sticking Solomon with all the cages to clean. But I didn't protest.

✦ ✦ ✦

The bath felt wonderful. Mrs. Greene's slave heated up water for me on the stove. I thought about just taking a cold bath, but I needed to scrub the grime off and that wasn't going to happen without some steam and some harsh lye soap. After I dried off, there were new boots and britches for me, too. My old shirt had also been replaced by a green print that would hide the dirt of the stables much better than the white one the orphanage had handed out on that last day.

I finally met Mrs. Greene at supper. She looked as sad as Caleb had described, kind of vacant and lost behind her eyes. She ate only a few bites off her plate, though she stared at its contents like all the great mysteries lay somewhere between the salt pork and the green beans. Gwendolyn tried to get Mrs. Greene to speak about new saddles and the other performers, but she didn't respond—not even to direct questions. It reminded me of Ma at the end, when she'd lost all the songs her voice knew. I did my best not to stare at Gwendolyn, but I didn't eat much trying to cut my food all proper like everyone else at the table. The silverware was heavy in my hand and shiny, with a fancy scroll pattern cut into it. I'd never touched anything so fine before, and it felt wrong to be using it just to stuff my face.

There was a lot of clatter of dishes and silverware

hitting plates until Mr. Greene took over and started to fill up the room with words. He talked about the invention of a new printing press and the price of ink and paper. Then he went into a whole tirade about spelling that bored me senseless, but I tried to seem interested since he had shown me such kindness. I kept yawning behind my hand though. The hot bath and good food was making me sleepy.

After the meal, Caleb and I went into his room. It was really just a closet with a bunk bed. It had no window, but it was his very own. The mattress was made of real feathers, and while he was pulling out his toys from a small box under his bed, I fell back into its fluffy softness. It felt like floating on a cloud compared to the scratchy, poking straw that I bedded down in each night.

After the warm bath and warm meal and the day spent out in the sunshine, I fell straight to sleep. It must've disappointed Caleb, but he left me there and I did not awake until I heard voices talking in the hall. The whole room was inky blackness, with only a finger of gaslight coming through the crack of the door. My mind spun around the corners of the room, trying to remember where I was.

"Why can't he just stay?" Caleb's voice sounded a bit whiney.

"We cannot ask any more of your mother right now," a deep voice answered quietly.

"But he sleeps in a stable, like a horse!" Caleb protested.

"I'll think on it, Caleb, but not tonight. Now, don't pester me on it further. Understood?"

"Yes, sir."

CHAPTER 17

I THANKED CALEB and the stump that was Mrs. Greene for supper and then raced back down to the stables. The show had already taken place and the animals were once again installed in their cages. Someone had done my work.

"I wondered if you might not be coming back," Solomon said behind me. His voice sounded sad and tired. Guilt filled me up.

"I . . . I'm sorry, Solomon. I fell asleep."

"Will you help me carry this basket up to the main deck?" he said, handing over a handle to a basket that was not as heavy as it was awkward. We walked in silence for a moment or two.

"What's it like working on that press?" Solomon asked.

"It's fine, I guess, though the tips of my fingers get sore from picking up those tiny letters," I answered.

"I know some letters," Solomon said quietly. I had never thought about him not being able to read. I mean, I guess I knew most slaves or even free Negroes probably couldn't read, but I just had never thought of it before. I remembered the shelves of glass jars in Solomon's potions closet. I remembered they had only pictures on their labels, no words.

"I could teach you the rest," I offered, unsure how he would take to me being his teacher, whether that would weigh on him, my years so few to his. The basket was awkward to manage, but slowly we made our way across the ring.

"I would like that very much." Solomon smiled then and looked me square in the eyes. It was the first time I'd seen real happiness cross over the old, worried lines that made up the map of his skin.

"I'll show you in the evenings when our chores are done, then," I offered, "and I can read to you, too, if we can find us some books."

"There's only one book that matters much to me."

"We'll start with that, then," I answered, knowing he meant the Good Book.

Just as we reached the deck we both froze—a large Negro man was standing in front of us, and his eyes opened wide when he saw us. His breeches and calico shirt were torn, and he did not have any shoes on his muddy feet. Solomon started to say something to the man, but he tore off around us and up the steps onto the balcony level. In our surprise, we dropped the basket, and the horseshoes and metal nails clanked out and skidded across the polished deck of the boat. Solomon and I dropped to our knees to clean up the mess.

"Do you think we should tell Hath—" My question was interrupted by a pack of baying hound dogs. They barked and whined along the bank of the river, and men on horseback followed behind them at a furious pace. Their lanterns swung light across the muddy bank and gleamed on the river like spirits chasing their souls. The dogs suddenly stopped in front of the ramp to the boat and howled furiously, like they'd treed a squirrel. The four men dismounted and ran aboard the *Palace*.

The oldest grabbed my shoulders and his face dropped within inches of mine. "You seen a boy run aboard?" His voice was loud, and his breath smelled of onions and whiskey. I shook my head no. I had seen a man, a giant scared man—but no boy.

"Are you lying to me?" My voice was lost. I shook my head again.

The other man lifted a lantern aloft and the muddy footprints of the Negro man made a path up the carpeted stairs. The men raced after the trail, but the smallest one of them slipped on a horseshoe and fell at my feet. He swore and righted himself, then scurried off after the others.

All the commotion caused Lord Hathaway to appear. He was not dressed but had on his nightshirt and a robe, looking like a boy who needed a story from his momma, not the intimidating owner of the ship.

"What in tarnation is going on out here?" he commanded.

"Slave catchers, sir," Solomon answered. "They chased a man on board." His voice sounded thin, like it might break.

"Hell's fire!" Lord Hathaway answered. "Which way did they go?" I pointed up the steps. His slippers made a *twup, twup, twup* sound as he ran up the steps.

I could hear the terrible ruckus the men were making in the grand amphitheater. The air felt swollen, like just before a big storm. Solomon stared off the bow of the boat, like he was stuck.

"How did you know he was an escaped slave?" I whispered to Solomon. I put my hand on his arm to pull him out of his thoughts. He stared at me for a moment like he didn't know me, but then he finally answered.

"Fear. Fear lit his eyes," he answered, and that broke the spell we both seemed to be in. We followed the yelling and ruckus up the stairs.

The slave catchers were exploring every dark corner of the balcony, turning over tables and tearing the red velvet drapes that hung on the dozens of windows. The lantern swung in the hand of the tallest man, and they called out to the slave as they worked. Hathaway kept yelling, "Don't damage my theater!" but the men ignored him.

"You might as well come out of your hiding spot," the one who had slipped demanded.

"You done caught now, boy. Come on out," another man teased.

"Don't make me any madder than I am!" said the largest, in a voice that could rattle hell.

A shadowy figure emerged from behind a large couch in a box seat. Everyone stopped like they were frozen. The large man looked defeated. His head hung like a schoolboy scolded by a teacher, and he walked slowly toward the light. As long as I know the sun, I will never forget what happened next.

Within steps of the lantern, the slave must've changed his mind, because he suddenly started to run, knocking down the man with the lantern. He bounded straight toward a window, his large body shattering the frame and glass. It sounded like the sky itself was cracking wide open and the whole ship would fall through the crack.

The fallen lantern exploded, and the flame licked the wool carpet like a wick. A pool of fire ignited and everyone turned from the window to face the flames. Solomon pulled one of the velvet curtains off a window and ran toward the fire. He threw it on top of the flames and then stomped on it, dousing the only light the room held.

The men retraced their steps best they could in the dark, and we followed them around the deck of the *Palace*. There was the slave, crumpled and bloody, his neck at a terrible angle from his body. Lord Hathaway tried to gain control of the situation.

"Which one of you shall pay for the damages?"

The men crossed their arms over their chests and glared down at us. The large man who had been knocked down when the slave jumped, bent down and sneered in Hathaway's face.

"We'll pay you nothing, you sniveling runt. If your boy hadn't lied, none of this would've happened." He towered over Hathaway, daring him to disagree.

"Whatever do you mean?" Hathaway asked, his voice high and unnatural.

"I mean"—the large man turned and pointed at

me—"this boy told us no one had run aboard. He lied. It is a crime to give harbor to runaway slaves." The other men took a step closer to me. Hathaway stepped backward but turned toward me.

"Is that true?" Lord Hathaway asked me, anger pinching his eyes into slits.

"I . . . I . . ." My voice faltered, and I wondered why Solomon did not try to defend me to these men. "I saw no boy. Just a man. They . . . They asked if a boy ran aboard." I tried to find Solomon so he would support my story, but he had disappeared.

"Smart aleck! Word-splitter. He knew exactly what I meant," the leader bellowed. The four men looked ready to pounce, like Lalla Rookh in his cage at mealtime.

"I didn't, I swear it." My voice cracked and I started crying. A man lay dead at my feet and it was my fault. Behind me came a voice I did not expect. It was Caleb's dad, Mr. Greene.

"Leave him be. He's but a boy himself," he said, putting a hand on my shoulder. Lord Hathaway came back to life with Mr. Greene beside him.

"Remove this trash, then, before his stain is permanent," Hathaway said, waving his hands dismissively over the scene.

The men grabbed the body of the slave, dragged

him off, and threw him over one of the horses. The dogs bayed, excited by their capture, and the troupe was slowly swallowed by the black night that had brought them.

Lord Hathaway started to question me further, but Greene spoke for me again.

"Enough. Let's deal with it in the morning." This unexpected kindness dammed the fountain of my tears. Greene's warm hand on my neck guided me back to the family stateroom, and he installed me into Caleb's bottom bunk with no further words of kindness or reprimand. The image of the dead slave flashed in my eyes. I thought about how Solomon had betrayed me in his silence. Anger and fear took turns with me all night, so sleep did not find me until the pale lavender light wedged its way through the open door.

CHAPTER

I WOKE UP LATE to find Caleb on the floor, playing with tin soldiers. He set them up into formations and then pitched marbles at them as if from a cannon. For just a split second I thought he was Zach all curled up on the floor and I was back home. I turned my face away to swallow the choking feeling in my throat. I missed my brother something awful, and though Caleb was better than no friend at all, he was not my brother. In all the world I wanted nothing more than to talk to my brother about last night's events.

"Are you finally awake?" Caleb asked, standing up from his toys.

"Yes."

"You missed breakfast already, but I snitched you a

couple of biscuits," he said, pulling out a handkerchief with several of them crumbling inside.

"I'm not hungry," I answered in a tone more nasty than I had intended.

"Are you sick? I've never seen you turn down food." Caleb smiled at me anyway, unaffected by my sour mood. He obviously had no idea what happened last night on the boat.

"I best get back down to the stables. There's always a bunch to do before the two o'clock Saturday show," I said, though I was not anxious to see Solomon.

"We're only having one show tonight," he answered, and then put his attention back onto the soldiers.

"How's that?" I wondered, as we had never missed a performance in all these weeks. Even when there were downpours the show still went on.

"Oh, every now and then Lord Hathaway gets a heart and lets people have Saturday to go to town and such."

"I've still got to help with the elephants."

"Nah. Come on, we'll go into the town mercantile and get some candy."

"Maybe later," I answered, though I didn't mean it. And I tried to smile as I walked out of Caleb's room. I did want to go to town, of course, but I had to go see to the elephants at least.

"I'll come down to the stables and get you, then."

* * *

The stables were clean, all of them. Someone must've helped move the animals into their show cages so that Solomon could clean them out. I wanted to avoid Solomon, not knowing what I might say to him out of anger. There could be no excuse for his leaving me at the mercy of those evil men. Still, going to town was a rare chance to spend the money I had earned, so I went to fetch my coins.

When I pushed aside the stable door, there was Solomon, building something out of scrap wood and ropes. I tried not to look at him, but went straight to my bedroll to get the coins.

"I worried on you last night," he said, almost like he was scolding me.

"Is that right?" I answered, annoyed.

"Yes. I didn't sleep for it." His voice was thick and his eyes tried to hold me there.

"Could've fooled me," I said, and then walked out of the stall. Anger for Solomon was still burning under my ribs. Who knows what would've happened if

Mr. Greene hadn't come along and gotten involved. I'm sure Hathaway would've turned me over to those men. Would they have killed me? Likely. Goose bumps crawled up my arm to think of it though it was the hottest day of the summer.

I walked along the bank of the river in these thoughts. A river rat, large as a dog, scurried into the underbrush. That's what Hathaway thinks of me. What hurt worse was knowing that Solomon did, too. I thought he was my friend.

It had been a long while since my feet had been on dry land, and it made me feel wobbly. I followed the path into the town. Memphis was busy. There were wagons going every which way and lots of boats docked along her shores. Walking toward me was a group of circus women in pairs, arm in arm, in their fanciest outfits. They looked like they were headed to a dance rather than coming back from shopping. Each lady carried a parcel or two, but as they passed me I heard them complain about the quality of the goods and how they would hold their money until they reached New Orleans.

The townswomen stopped and stared as the fancy circus women walked by them in front of the shops. In comparison, their ragged calicoes and plain shawls made them look like they were just out of an orphanage.

Disapproval dripped from their squinted eyes and I heard words laced with venom whispered between them. I had not realized women spoke about each other like this. Perhaps it was jealousy, but it seemed deeper than that.

I remembered how bright I thought the makeup and frillery that made up a circus performer was at first, but now their colors did not surprise me. At first it seemed harsh, kind of like the sound of the calli compared to the orchestra. They were both considered music, but one felt more like it was meant for attention. I'm sure the spinster sisters would be aghast at the lavish wardrobes and fanciness of the women, but Lord, they were Quakers—everything was too fancy for them.

The mercantile was packed with customers, all waiting for service. The front of the store held great glass jars of every variety of candy, and I could get a bagful for fifteen cents. In a corner I spotted marbles. Real glass marbles like we always talked about having, me and Zach, instead of the pebbles we tried to shape ourselves. I rubbed the coins together in my pocket and wished Zach was beside me. I would give him one of the coins, I swear it. Though I was getting too old for such things and didn't have time to play with them really, I bought the marbles and a bag of candy besides. I still had some money leftover, too, and I tied the coins back in the rag for a different day. I already missed knowing I had those coins, and without Zachary to play them with me, owning the marbles didn't give me near the thrill I'd always dreamed it would.

I saw Caleb walking toward town with his ma and sister, and he looked surprised to see me coming the other way.

"I tried to get you. Solomon said you had left already," Caleb said.

"I wanted to hurry," I lied, knowing I just didn't want to talk to him or anybody else.

"See you tomorrow?" Caleb asked, hopefully, and I felt guilty for leaving him behind.

"I can't tomorrow," I lied. Sunday was the one day I could get away if I wanted.

"All right, then. I guess I'll see you Monday," he answered, disappointed again, walking slowly behind his ma and sister, his eyes trying to follow me down the narrow path. I slipped into an alley to avoid his stare. I could've said I'd come get him for some fishing or that I'd see him on Monday. But my lips remained stuck together, and I could not give him what I knew he wanted. Nasty, I think, is my middle name.

Hunger pulled on the bottom of my belly, so I

found a nearby restaurant and ordered the breakfast special. I was sopping up my soft egg yolk with my left hand and shoving a sausage in with my right when I nearly choked on it all from a sudden realization. My left hand was working at feeding me with the same power as my right. Over the weeks it had felt stronger, and somewhere along the way it had healed without me much noticing. Maybe I could've found a place with Zach after all. Maybe some farmer would've taken us both on if I hadn't been lame in one arm. I guess I'd never know. I felt like I had lost both Zachary and Solomon and never had I felt so alone in my whole life. I even let myself miss Ma. It felt like a hand was squeezing my heart dry of its blood. My eyes filled with tears—right there at the restaurant counter— and I was suddenly repulsed by all the food in front of me. The waitress came up and saw my face.

"Honey, can I get you something? You look like someone just walked over your grave."

"No, ma'am," I answered, and abandoned my plate, leaving plenty for the tip beside my napkin. I did stuff the two biscuits in my handkerchief for later. The sun beat down on the top of my head so I found a bench under a magnolia tree to think. I took out two of the marbles and rolled them in my fingers and tried as I might to call up Zach's face. It was getting softer around the edges of my memory. I could remember details—his moppy hair, the way his teeth marched in a straight line between his smiling lips. But when I could not picture his whole face anymore, it made me feel frozen. Lost. When a wind picked up I realized that I'd been sitting on that bench for hours. Though I did not want to see Solomon or that boat where that man had thrown his life out a window, I picked myself up and went there, for I had nowhere else to go.

◆　◆　◆

I shared the bits left from my biscuit with the always-curious trunk of Little Bet. The tip of her trunk was moist like a puppy's nose. But she acted more like a starving hound dog the way she was always sniffing out any little tidbit from the sawdust or hay. She slipped her trunk under my hair (which was in sore need of a trim) and it tickled me. Despite my attempt to stay in a foul mood, it made me laugh and it felt good to have some of the seriousness of the last hours melt away. If I didn't know any better, I'd swear she could tell I needed cheering up.

Little Bet hadn't learned anything yet that an audience would want to see, but Mendeley worked with her some nearly every day. After I spent some time with Little Bet, I went to check out the other animals that were so rarely in their cages while I was around. Only their strange rumblings and calls in the night were familiar to me, like a haunting.

The three tigers shared a cage, and they slept, peaceful and easy on their sides in the scattering of hay. The lions, too, slept, even the great male lion, Lalla Rookh, whose mane looked like an extra animal tied around his shoulders, like a woman's furry shawl. I studied the golden landscape of his muscles to make sure he was breathing, so still was his body. His paw was still not quite healed from the terrible night of the feedings.

The monkeys hopped from one dead branch to another inside their small quarters. They bared their teeth at me and spit orange rind in my direction. I didn't stay long with the monkeys, because their screeching was as unnerving as squeaky chalk. The great black bear, Titus, paced around the confines of his cage, his head swinging back and forth like a metronome. Slobber flung out of his mouth, and his eyes seemed to jiggle inside their sockets, not focusing on anything. He looked more like those odd men who talked to garbage I'd sometimes see on the streets in Pittsburgh than a wild bear.

Behind me a voice broke my thoughts. "It's the bars made him gone mad." Solomon's voice was quiet but sure. I didn't answer him, though I longed to ask him how he knew such a thing. Wasn't it finer for a bear to have meat brought to him twice a day than go starving in a forest? Solomon stood next to me, his hands on the bars of the cage. I stiffened at his presence, having avoided him in my anger.

"He has meat and a bed," I answered, finally annoyed, "more than many people." I tried to say it like it didn't matter, but my voice shook and betrayed me.

"But he is shackled to a man's will, so he is but a slave," Solomon answered.

"He's a wild beast!" I said, irritated, not because I really believed what I said, but because I wanted to disagree with Solomon at any price.

"There is nothing wild in him . . . nor nothing free."

"You are free!" I grabbed Solomon's arm, my anger tipping out at last, "and yet you said nothing. Nothing to defend me last night. I might've ended up in the river again," I answered, and my voice cracked.

And the picture of the broken man flooded into my mind again. I stood in his face, burning with my feelings. He dropped his head and looked at his worn boots.

"I am sorry," Solomon answered, stuffing his hands in his pockets. "I could not risk it." His voice sounded as though he might cry. It shocked me, but I still pressed him.

"Risk what? You are a free man." I crossed my arms over my chest to keep myself from crumpling into a heap, so raw did I feel.

"Those slave catchers wanted a prize to deliver," he answered, putting his hands on my shoulders and looking me squarely in the face. "I'm sorry. I could not risk it to be me." His voice shook with fear, something I had not heard before.

"But the man they chased died! They took his body as proof," I yelled, and turned away from him, not wanting him to see the tears in my eyes.

"Do you think they would not have exchanged me for him? Their reward would be much higher for a slave who can pick cotton than for one that must be buried."

"Oh," I answered, still trying to let his words sink into my brain.

"They deal in flesh. They have no mercy. No honor," he finished quietly.

"I had not thought of that," I answered, finally understanding and not knowing what else to say. I would've hidden, too. I looked back at the bear pacing around and around his small quarters.

"Slavery is a cage with invisible bars," Solomon said quietly, "and I lived inside it for forty years." We stood together silently for some time.

"What was the worst part?" I dared to ask him.

"It wasn't the beatings, leastways not for me." His voice choked. "It was the sellings."

I didn't know what to say, so I nodded and put my arm on his shoulder. He looked down at me and his eyes were near to spilling over.

"I'm sorry, Solomon. So sorry." Was I apologizing for having been so angry with him or for not understanding one ounce what slavery meant? Either way, it was not enough.

He nodded and turned toward our stall. Inside I could see what Solomon had been working on earlier in the day. Pushed against opposing walls were rough framed beds. The mattresses were still hay, but it was fresh and tucked inside a striped ticking. The mattresses were supported by a weave of ropes and knots. It was not Caleb's duck-feather bed, but it was cozy, and it was mine. Between the two beds stood a table and a damaged wicker chair from the ticket holders' seats. The last spoonful of my fear and anger fell to the floor between these new beds. Solomon was doing his best to make amends, and so would I.

For the rest of the afternoon we passed the bag of candy between us as I read aloud from Genesis. "In the beginning" will forever taste like peppermint to me.

CHAPTER

FOR DAYS PEOPLE SPOKE of nothing but New Orleans. The freaks, the printers, even the slaves talked about what they would do once we arrived in the fairest of all Southern cities, the crescent and crown jewel of the river. Great debates and arguments about where the best food and the best accommodations could be found popped up over every meal and task. It seemed most everyone had an opinion on the Crescent City. Mostly, though, everyone was excited at the chance of being docked somewhere for a few weeks to stay in fancy rooms that did not rock or jolt. Most of them would, anyway. Solomon and I and a few others would remain on the *Palace* or the *Attaboy* while a slick coat of paint freshened up the already-worn places that so many thousands of visitors had caused.

The city was unbelievable. Firstly, because of the number of steamboats and flatboats docked along the harbor. Hundreds of them! We were still the largest, of course, but we were quite used to being the only ship in a whole town. I didn't get to travel much off board, but when I did, I was stunned to hear a new language, sometimes on every block. Even those who were supposed to be speaking my tongue had such a strange rhythm to their words it didn't make sense, leastways not to me. Solomon had been a slave not far from here, he said, on a cotton plantation. New Orleans, he told me, had every kind of person from every kind of nation. I believed him.

On the sixth day at dock, we were printing handbills and sheets to post around the city when Lord Hathaway barged in, his hands flapping like a chicken's wings, looking uncharacteristically foolish and unkempt.

"Stop! Stop printing!" Hathaway yelled, his voice pinched.

We all stopped and stared at him.

"I have sent word to everyone to return to the *Palace* immediately!" Hathaway was nearly out of control of his senses.

Greene looked up from his work, surprised. "We're not ready. We have two more days before our opening performance."

"There will be no opening here! It is the yellow jack!" With each word his voice got a little higher. The room froze. Greene dropped the sheets he held. They fluttered to the floor and he ran from the room, Caleb after him. Lord Hathaway, flustered and speaking like a madman under his breath, dismissed us to help anywhere we might.

"We leave tonight!" he announced again, his voice like a young girl's. Though I was mightily confused and pressed to know what had him so scared, I did not ask. I, too, raced from the press room, to find Solomon.

I searched in all the stalls until I finally found him brushing down Roman. Rushing into the stable I spooked Roman, and he reared up at me. Still the questions began spilling from me as fast as I could make them. "Solomon, what is yellow jack? What is going on? Why must we push off tonight?"

"Whoa!" Solomon calmed the stallion with his steady hand and then answered me. "Whoa to you, too, Owen. Slow down, now, and I'll answer all your questions." His voice calmed the panic I had roosting under my ribs. He continued brushing the stallion, whose flesh rippled and whose one eye followed me as I paced around.

"Explain it!" I demanded, frustrated with his slow pace.

"It's the fever," he said quietly. "As ways to leave this world go, it may be the worst."

"Why?" I asked, wanting and yet not wanting to know. I grabbed another brush and joined him in brushing down the great stallion. The motion calmed me some.

"Your body be racked in pain and your blood tries to get out whatever way it can—even the eyes." I stopped brushing and stared at him. It sounded too foul to be true.

"Will we get it?" I asked.

"I had it once as a boy, so they say I cannot have it again."

"Will I?" I was afraid for his answer, but he did not hesitate.

"Unlikely. They think it is the bad air that brings it out, and we have been aboard the ship the whole while," he said, pitching the brush into its bucket. Outside Roman's stall workers were bustling around like the place was on fire. Word had obviously reached everyone else.

"What about the performers and workers who left the *Palace*?" I asked, worrying now about Caleb and his family, who had spent near a week in the grand St. Charles Hotel. I had been jealous not to get to see the hotel that took up its own city block, but now, suddenly I was glad I had not.

"God himself knows," Solomon answered. "Now, we have a week's worth of work to do before we push off tonight." I could see his mind working out the list of chores that would need to be accomplished. Everything seemed louder than it needed to be—the hammering, the hauling, the stacking. The animals, too, picked up on the intensity around them and soon they added their roars, bellows, and trumpets to the intense atmosphere. Workers scurried everywhere in the last-minute preparations and chattered nervously about what they had learned of the foul disease. People who never spoke to each other were suddenly tied together by this terrible event. I tried not to listen about how many people had died in old epidemics or details about the dreadful disease, but I couldn't help it. Fear and panic darted among everyone's words.

Though my thoughts were as crowded as my old orphanage, I did not get the chance to ask any more questions. We loaded. And loaded. And loaded. We loaded crates of food and feed until I thought we might could well feed all of New Orleans for a month. I know it was rattlebrained, but I tried not to take deep breaths just in case there were any bad humors floating around inside the barge, too. After midnight the *Palace* was pushed off the shore and the faithful *Attaboy* towed her out into the open waters of the Gulf. We were to head east toward Mobile, Alabama, and then up the Ouachita and Red rivers in the hope that the fever would not follow us.

Solomon and I climbed atop the *Palace*, though the night was cool on the open water. As the lights and panic of New Orleans fell away, a great silence drifted over the ship. Never before had I seen so much water. I knew of the sea, of course, from books and stories, but I was not prepared for it or the blanket of stars above it. We both leaned back into the gentle rocking of the ship, our heads propped on our hands and our weary backs finally at rest.

"I heard tell the armless man and the fat woman did not board the *Palace*," I said.

"He has the fever," Solomon answered, "and she would not leave him."

"Won't she likely die, too?" I asked. One of the things I'd heard was that about half of those who got the fever died of it.

"She may," he answered.

A quiet fell between us and I thought of how I'd left Zach on the train. Abandoned him to a fate I did not know. It felt cowardly now. Nellie, the fat lady, faced a terrible death but stood beside her friend. I left my brother to find a family on his own and I faced only rejection.

"I should not have left him," I said aloud.

"Who?" Solomon asked.

"My brother." And then I told Solomon all the words I had held these long months. I told him that I was a coward when I most needed to be brave.

"You're no coward, Owen," he said, "but I am."

I did not know what to say to him so I let the silence engulf us. It was a few minutes of the waves gently rocking the boat before he continued.

"I left my woman and children behind me."

"You had children?" I asked, surprised.

"I had three."

Afraid to press him, I waited. Finally Solomon continued. "Master rented out my work with animals. I cured animals and slaves with my teas and ointments."

He coughed then, and sat up, wrapping his strong, lean arms around his legs as he continued. I, too, sat up to listen.

"I could keep a bit of what I earned each week. I bought my freedom this way. But once I had it I fell in love with the bottle. I spent every extra coin on drinking."

A breeze picked up then and goose flesh crawled up my arms. I shivered but did not want to leave Solomon. I clenched my teeth so they would not chatter and waited for the words I knew would come.

"I tried to drown the memory of slavery. The whippings. The auctions. The way my momma died in the fields. But it did not drive my past from me. Alcohol became my master and I had sold myself into its bondage."

"I never thought of it that way," I answered, realizing for the first time that my own father had been a slave to the bottle, too. It had cost me my whole family. The anchor of hate I had carried for my father all this time slipped away.

"When I finally sobered I lived on the streets that I might save more money and faster."

"I'm sorry, Solomon."

"None as sorry as me. When I went back for them, they were gone. Sold in separate directions." His voice broke, and he rested his heavy head in his arms.

"Maybe I can help you find your family," I offered, not knowing what else to say to my friend.

"Find your own," he answered solemnly. "Find your own."

We stayed there in silence for a long while. I'd hated my pa for so long that it felt like an anchor chained around me, but I could feel it loosen somehow, knowing Solomon's story. I hated the alcohol instead and swore that none should ever pass my lips. And I swore silently against slavery, too. I guess I was turning out Quaker after all.

Solomon stood up and I knew to follow him. It

would be a long day tomorrow like all the others. Just as I began to throw my leg over the ladder, we heard the voice of Hathaway and two ticket men below. Solomon pulled me back onto the roof, and we squatted down lest they see us. Hathaway was giving directions, and unlike his usual boastful self, they were given in words just above a whisper. I strained to hear them over the lap of the waves against the boat.

"Do not hesitate on this," Hathaway said. "If someone shows signs of it, send them overboard."

The two henchmen nodded, coughed, and each gave a quiet "Yes, sir."

"We must not dock with anyone ill or we will be turned away. Word would spread that we are the Pestilence Palace. Now go."

The two men headed off around the deck of the ship, and Hathaway himself stood there for a long time, smoking a slender cigarette. When he finally went off to bed, Solomon and I climbed down with this terrible knowledge between us.

CHAPTER

I DREAMED OF THE FAT WOMAN and the armless man in the same hospital bed. Their faces, red with fever, the white sheets spotted with dried blood. Then, the room was filled with monkeys. The *Palace*'s monkeys were squawking, as they do, and tearing apart the room. Only that's when Solomon woke me because the monkeys were really squawking, having gotten out, and were now inside the aviary, torturing the exotic birds.

The light cast from our meager lantern was nowhere near good enough to catch the shadowy devils as they jumped from one perch to the next. Finally, I fetched an apple and sat down on the floor and began eating it. The floor of the aviary was scattered with feathers, the bright plumes creating a kaleidoscope on the bare floor. Solomon came back with a rope and shook his head at me sitting on the floor. But the pair of monkeys plunked down in front of me, holding out their hands for a slice of apple. I gave each a piece and they let me swing them up into my arm, as if they were my own babes. But when I stood up I could not gain my balance. I felt as if I would pitch forward and land on top of the little beasts. Solomon grabbed me under the shoulders to steady me and together we put the little demons back in their cage.

When they were installed, Solomon turned all his attention to me. He felt my face with his bare hands and stared into my eyes. Again, I felt like my knees didn't belong beneath me and I buckled into Solomon's arms. He carried me back to my bed. I must have passed out because the next time I opened my eyes, the stall was filled with light. It seemed gray and frightening.

"Good Lord, have mercy," Solomon said as he stood over me. And I knew. The fever had found me. I ached. My knees, my elbows, every place I could bend felt as though someone had used a hammer on them. Solomon sat me up and forced a bitter tea down my throat. When I gagged on it, he brought more. Time disappeared.

I thought at first that my ears were filled with the screams of the dying, so loud was the sound growing inside my head. But Solomon told me it was a storm brewing on the sea. The boat pitched and swayed, making me lose the contents of my stomach over and again. My head, too, felt like it was being pressed by a vise and felt three times its natural size. I was sure that had I a mirror, I would have seen a new kind of freak—one with a giant ball for a face. Finally, sleep took me, only to haunt me with dreams of my worst days. Images strung like beads into my fevered head, though their order was scrambled:

I was back on the orphan train with Zachary, but this time he knew my plan and kept tugging on my arm, saying, "Don't go, Owen! Don't leave me." I could hear the voices of the children singing all around us, hopeful and scrubbed in their new clothes. But Zach was dirty, smeared with tears, and in his old, torn clothes.

Then I was back in our old apartment with Momma. She was baking cookies with cinnamon and I could smell and taste them. She was humming to herself and had a secret smile on her face. But when I reached for a cookie, they turned into marbles rolling around the plate.

Then my brain swirled again and I was standing over my pa just as I truly found him, dead as stone. He'd stumbled in his drunken stupor and cracked his skull on the fireplace bricks. His blood like syrup on my fingers. Momma in the doorway, screaming, and Zach curled up like a dog in the corner.

Then I was pulling Zach off Momma while he begged her not to sign us over to the orphanage. "At least you will eat here," she said. In my mind these words repeated again and again. "At least you will eat here. At least you will eat here. At least you . . ."

"I would rather starve and stay together!" I screamed at last.

"Shhhhh." Solomon settled me back into my bed. "It's the fever. Take this tea." His voice was soothing and warm. I clung to his arm though my eyes saw my momma before me, not Solomon.

A cool rag was draped across the fire of my face.

"It's all right now, Owen, Solomon's got you. You rest now, you rest."

The next time I woke I was in total darkness, but I could hear the clank of bottles and the ship being tossed around, almost in circles. I did not know if it was the storm or the fever, but I pulled the blankets around me and settled back inside the pallet that had been made for me behind tall whiskey barrels. Why had Solomon moved me inside his potions closet? I did not know, but trying to sort out my thoughts made me tired again, so I slept.

When I woke again my head was clear. Still, I was in the dark, but I managed to stumble my way across the small room and out into the bright light of the day. Solomon saw me immediately.

"Are you well?" he asked me, his hand immediately seeking out the skin of my forehead.

"I think so," I answered, though I felt weak and worn.

"Your fever is gone." He smiled at me and I could see the worry untie in his brow.

"I'm starving," I answered, certain of this. Solomon stacked up blankets behind me and settled me back.

"You've got to take it slow. It's been five days since you've had anything but tea." He went to the corner of the room and started putting together a small plate of food. My mouth felt dry as paper.

"Five days?" I managed to whisper.

"Five," he answered again, and brought a small plate with slices of a bruised red apple, a small piece of bread with jam, and more tea. I thought I might eat the plate, too.

"Are we in Mobile?" I remembered now that we were supposed to land the day after we left New Orleans.

"No. We are still in the open sea." He picked up the tea and pressed it to my lips. Solomon looked haggard, like he'd been awake the whole five days. Maybe he had.

"Why?" I asked, needing to feel like I was back from my nightmares. Needing to feel grounded in the now.

"They had to cut the *Attaboy* loose during the storm. We nearly shipwrecked into each other for the winds." That sounded pretty exciting and a part of me wished I hadn't missed all the action. But what happened when you separated a barge from its tow?

"Are we adrift?" Would we be lost in the open water forever?

I fell back asleep before hearing Solomon's answer. When I awoke again, Solomon fed me and then helped me get to my feet.

We walked toward our stable, Solomon's arm under my elbow, guiding me. Though my legs were weak, it felt good to be up. The sun poured in through the high windows of the stable and the light made me cover my eyes. It was hard to believe a storm had ever happened. The breeze from the water was warm and cool at the same time. The place was oddly empty of workers and even the animals seemed quiet.

* * *

"Where is everyone?" I asked, afraid of what he might say.

"Many are gone," he answered, turning away from

me. He coughed and wiped his eyes with the back of his hand. He was fighting tears.

"What do you mean?"

"Lost. Lost to the sea or to the fever." He broke then and silent tears streamed down his worn face. We stumbled back to our own stable and both collapsed on the beds he had made. Solomon was asleep almost immediately, and the sound of his soft snoring was an odd comfort to me. He slept straight through until morning.

All through the night my sleep was fitful as I thought about all the people I had met and wondered who had survived. Caleb, especially, pressed on my thoughts. Caleb and his family. I did not want to wake Solomon but was tortured not knowing the truth. Of course, if we were cut away from the *Attaboy*, there was probably no way to know who survived on the other ship.

In the early light Solomon and I explored what was left of the *Palace*. Shards of glass glinted in the bright morning sun. Tools, wheelbarrows, even feed lay up against the far wall, as if in a snowdrift.

"The animals, too?" I asked. They were too quiet.

"Most are fine," he answered quickly, "though we're running low on food."

"Is Little Bet okay?"

"Yes, yes, she made it," he answered, and then we were suddenly inside the amphitheater itself. I could not believe it. All of the glass windows were shattered and the seats were covered with seaweed and rotting fish and shards of glass. The circus ring itself was a small pond, holding nearly a foot of water inside the sturdy permanent structure. Paintings were smeared, chairs turned over, and the beautiful velvet curtains hung in rags.

"What did Lord Hathaway say of this?" I asked, and then remembered the last of Hathaway's words, about throwing victims of the fever overboard before we landed. I realized, suddenly, why I had been tucked inside Solomon's closet of remedies. Of course, he was hiding me from Hathaway and his men so I would not be cast out to sea. I shivered to realize how close I had come to being lost myself.

"He blames me," Solomon answered, his voice low and shaking with anger and humiliation.

"He blames you for the storm?" I asked. It made no sense. Solomon could not control the seas. I followed Solomon back to our stable.

"For the damage," Solomon answered, picking his way through the wreckage that littered the floor. "I should have covered the windows and nailed all the heavy things down."

"Do you think it would've helped? To block out the windows?"

"Yes. Maybe. Who's to know? I was not prepared for such a storm," he answered heavily, and finally sank down into his bed. Immediately he fell into a slumber, and I covered him with the frayed wool blanket at his feet. I, too, was suddenly tired again and lay down on my bunk and slept, gratefully, without dreams.

CHAPTER

IN THE MORNING we found ourselves docked back in New Orleans, having been towed, finally, by a smaller ship that spotted us adrift. The *Attaboy* was also docked in the Crescent City, about a half mile down the bank, but it had fared not much better than the *Palace* herself. The railings of the second story had been completely ripped away and all the glass windows were shattered. Worry over Caleb and his family was like a sack I carried around with me but could not put down. I tried to get to their stateroom, but the external stairway was missing entirely. I was looking for a way to climb up to their door, when a man interrupted my thoughts.

"Are you looking for your young friend?" asked a

Negro man who had been one of the printers. I had not learned his name.

"Yes. Do you know where the Greene family is?"

"Three of them went back to that fancy hotel."

It felt like someone stabbed a stick into my throat. There were four people in Caleb's family, not three. Who had died from the yellow jack? The man hurried aboard the *Attaboy* with his heavy box of supplies. Nausea washed over me, thinking of facing the Greene family. But I had to know. What if it was Caleb?

Though it had only been two weeks since we fled, it felt like I had aged twenty years. It took me over an hour to find the St. Charles, though it was an enormous landmark. It had pillars and columns and a fancy-dressed Negro at the entrance opening the doors for the guests climbing out of the carriages. He even opened the door for me though I obviously did not belong, in my tattered clothes.

It took me a full five minutes to get the nerve to ask at the front desk for the Greene family. They would not let me go directly to their room but sent someone with a note that I was in the lobby. I wanted to sit on the fancy furniture—it was even more elegant than anything on the *Palace*—but I was afraid they might throw me out onto the street if I soiled the cream-colored silks. I leaned against a wall instead, resting my still-wobbly sea legs. While waiting, I studied the clothes and severe faces of the wealthy people staying at the hotel. They did not, I noticed, look any happier than anyone else despite their fine clothing and jewelry. The plague did not care if you had money or not.

"Owen, I'm glad you survived the storm and the fever," Mrs. Greene said in a formal way when she found me in the lobby. She motioned for me to follow her but not before her eyes had trolled over my shabby appearance. I had not expected her to come for me at all. On the way to the third floor she did not ask me any questions but kept her gloved hands clasped formally in front of her dress. Too afraid to ask questions myself, I stuffed my hands in my pockets.

When she opened the door, Caleb jumped up from the sofa and ran over to me. He hugged me tighter than I expected.

"I was so worried about you, Owen!" His voice was high and excited. Again, he reminded me of Zach. They might've been school chums given the chance, I thought.

"Me too," I said, though I was still worried about who was missing. Then Gwendolyn came out of one of the rooms, but she looked frail and was dressed only in a robe. That was the third Greene. I realized that Mr. Greene must've died, and I swallowed a hard lump in my throat. I hadn't liked him at first, but he did save me the night of the escaped slave. These thoughts raced around my head.

"Oh! I didn't realize we had company!" Gwendolyn turned and went back into the bedroom.

I thought it was an odd thing to be thinking about with your pa dead, but girls were odd creatures for sure. Who would ever understand them? Gwendolyn had looked pale, but neither Caleb nor his momma looked any different to me. I tried to look around the many corners in the room to see if Mr. Greene's body was laid out for a funeral. But, of course, if he had died of the jack, they wouldn't have kept his body for burial.

"Are you looking for something?" asked Mrs. Greene.

"Uh, I'm . . . no. I was just wondering if, if I might have a glass of water."

"Of course. You probably haven't eaten anything much, have you?"

"No, ma'am."

"I'll order up some food then for you, too."

"Thank you," I answered, really meaning it.

✦   ✦   ✦

Caleb sat down on the sofa. I couldn't do it. I was just too grubby. I sat down on the floor in front of the carved tea table.

"I have a thousand questions for you!" he said. "Where were you during the storm? How many people got sick from the fever? Did anything wash overboard?"

I couldn't stand it anymore. "Caleb, did your pa die, too?" I asked, and my voice broke, allowing myself to think about my own pa for a second.

"Oh, no!" Caleb answered, and patted my shoulder. "He's up in Pennsylvania."

A great relief swept over me at the news.

We traded stories for the next couple of hours. Caleb's father had gone to Philadelphia to find land. The Greenes would be breeding and training horses instead of performing on them. Apparently Gwendolyn had nearly died with the yellow jack fever, and it had brought Mrs. Greene back to life. She was not prepared to lose another child. She nursed Gwendolyn for three days straight, washing her constantly with chilled water to cool her fever.

Caleb also told me the details from the storm on the *Attaboy*. It had taken more of a beating than the *Palace* because it was so much smaller. Water had poured into their stateroom and they had locked themselves inside a pantry closet so as not to get washed out to sea. That's when they had decided to leave the circus, if they survived. Others, I learned, weren't so lucky. Two equestrians, Mr. Thimble, and the Colossal Cowgirl all drowned. The Lion King had died of the fever. Though they had not been my friends, I felt like I knew them. I swallowed hot tears.

"Strange to think on it, ain't it?" Caleb said solemnly.

"Don't seem real, none of it," I answered, feeling like I might not ever wake up from this nightmare after all.

"The *River Palace* is defunct," Mrs. Greene said, placing a tray of sandwiches on the table. "I heard it shall be auctioned for debts, what's left of it anyway," she said. Her voice seemed cold, like ice. Did she not feel for those who lost everything? Or was this her way of surviving?

The *Palace* had become my home. I had nowhere else to go. I felt like I was cut loose again, out to sea, adrift. I had no home, no other prospects. My hands went cold from the fear of not knowing what might become of me.

Caleb started to reach for the sandwiches, but Mrs. Greene smacked away his hand and said, "Caleb, Owen needs to bathe before he eats. Show him to the facilities."

I was dying to dive into the food but I didn't want to be rude, so I followed Caleb. Mrs. Greene called after us, "See if you have some clothes for him as well."

"He won't fit into my britches. He's a head taller than me!"

{ 154 }

After my scrubbing, I was given clothes that apparently belonged to Mr. Greene. They were not too ridiculous as I had grown a great deal since boarding the *Palace*. I tried to eat politely, but it was difficult with my stomach suddenly feeling like a hungry pit. Caleb picked at his food, but I finished every morsel of mine. When Mrs. Greene left the room, he switched our plates and I finished his, too.

When Mrs. Greene came back into the room to collect our plates, she looked at me differently.

"Why, Owen, what are your plans now that the *Palace* is to be sold?" I was surprised by the directness of her question.

"I want to find my brother," I said aloud, when I thought I was only thinking it.

"Whatever do you mean?" asked Mrs. Greene.

"My brother went off on one of them orphan trains, and I'd like to know where he ended up," I answered.

"Why didn't you go with him?" Caleb asked.

"It's a long story, Caleb."

"We have time," Mrs. Greene nudged gently. Her face looked softer now somehow. Like maybe she was seeing me for more than a heap of dirt. Gwendolyn, too, came out of the bedroom and sat on a chair to listen.

"It started when my pa died," I began, and I told

them the whole story about how Momma had to give us up so's we could eat after Pa died. I told them about the Home for Destitute and Friendless Youth, the sorriest place anyone would ever want to land. And speaking of landing, I suggested they never fall out of a great elm tree, neither, because it might take you on a path you'd just never imagine. I described Zachary and how Caleb reminded me so much of him and about the spinster sisters, too. And I told how Solomon had saved me from being fish food. Also how Mr. Greene had saved me the night of the slave escape, too. That I needed a lot of saving. They sat and listened the whole time, Mrs. Greene making me pause every now and then while she fetched more tea and food.

"And now I need saving again," I ended, hoping I wasn't being too forward but realizing the Greenes could help me more than anybody else I knew.

"Well," said Mrs. Greene, "we will need a stable boy. You could work for us until you find your brother."

Relief swept over me, mixed with sadness, too. I would miss the *Palace*. And Solomon. I knew I didn't really have a choice. I accepted as graciously as I could muster.

"I appreciate that offer, ma'am. Yes, thank you."

"I'm sure Mr. Greene would be fine with that arrangement"—she patted my shoulder—"and you can travel with us in a few days."

"Thank you," I said again, but my mind was back on the *Palace*, wondering what would become of Solomon and the animals.

"It'd be almost like we're brothers!" said Caleb. "Ma, could Owen spend the night here with us?"

"I don't think that's a good—"

"Please!" Caleb begged. "I ain't had no one to play with in weeks!"

I stared at my feet, uncomfortable in front of them both.

"No, Caleb," I added in. "I need to report back to Solomon and see what needs to be done."

The room fell silent for a moment, but then Mrs. Greene spoke up with a quiet authority.

"He's obviously a fine Negro," Mrs. Greene answered, "but you need not answer to him so. I'll send word to the ship of our arrangement. You can go collect your things tomorrow." I was relieved to have someone take over my situation for me, so I agreed, but I was torn, too, making these plans without at least talking to Solomon first. Maybe I could convince the Greenes tomorrow to take Solomon back to Pennsylvania. Maybe if I told the part about how Solomon saved me from Hathaway's hench-men, they'd know he was worth taking with them. I didn't sleep much that night, working on my strategy to get Solomon a job, too.

CHAPTER

I MEANT TO GET BACK to the *Palace* in the morning. But my body, still recovering from yellow jack, slept until it was near dinnertime. Mrs. Greene insisted that I eat first before she'd let me leave. Then she made a few chores for Caleb and I to do and I couldn't refuse her after she'd been so kind. When a whole roast with new potatoes was delivered, I knew I would wait until after dinner to leave.

Then Caleb insisted that I play cards with him for a bit longer, and then it was dark outside already. Mrs. Greene relented much easier about me staying one extra night, saying that Caleb had been easier to tolerate when not pestering her.

"I'll send word to that tyrant Lord Hathaway." I

wanted to mention Solomon again, but it always seemed to make her angry, so I let the words rot inside my lips.

"Yes, ma'am. Can you help me send a telegram to Pittsburgh?"

"To the spinster ladies? Do you think they'll know where your brother was adopted?"

"I hope so," I answered, not really knowing if they would or not.

"We'll just send it down to the front desk and they'll take care of it."

"Terrific," I answered, though I didn't feel terrific about it. I sat down, awkward with a pencil, and tried to ask in as few words as possible about Zach. Mrs. Greene helped me cut words and letters to save money, then took it to the lobby herself. My stomach was in knots thinking that I would learn what had happened to Zach. Solomon was right—I had to know what happened to my brother. Because I had slept so much of the day away, I tossed like a ship in the bed that night. Caleb and I shared a large bed, but I felt bad for keeping him awake, so I finally found a book and read until a telegram was slipped under the door in the early hours of the morning. My hands shook as I opened the cream-colored paper:

We adopted Zachary STOP He misses you
STOP Our home is yours STOP

Please come back STOP

Zach was with the spinsters! I wondered how and
when they had adopted him. Maybe they felt sorry for
him because no one wanted him on the orphan train.
They did always dote on him so. My brain swirled with
possibilities. I couldn't imagine the spinster sisters
were offering me a place now. I needed time to think
and I didn't want to talk to Caleb or Mrs. Greene. I
decided to find Solomon and ask him what he thought
I should do. Had he already found employment with a
new circus?

Fires burned on corners along the streets between
the hotel and the docks. I heard a bellman say that they
thought the fires would help burn off whatever was
causing the great scourge of yellow jack upon the city.
Now that I'd had it, I didn't have to worry about being
outside. Caleb was not allowed to leave the hotel, and
he was going a bit daft being cooped up with his momma
and sister.

All along the streets were funeral processions. Caskets on open carts and families dressed in black, walking and sometimes wailing, behind them. The caskets

were of every shape and size and design. Some intricately carved and painted with cherubs, others plain cedar boxes. I saw one so small I could tuck it under my arm. I finally decided to cut through the alleys instead so that I wouldn't have to see any more.

The *Palace* looked like a ragged box bobbing in the water. All the dozens of windows were cracked and the fancy scrollwork gone. It was sorrowful to see her look like this. I boarded her with a heavy rock for a heart.

It felt ghostly without the sprightly calli music and bells that had become so much a part of my life on the ship. Down the red-carpeted stairs I went, into the main arena and across the soggy sawdust floor. It was still a shock to see the auditorium shredded from its former glory. There was no one around, which seemed eerie after the thousands who streamed through her doors most every night.

I looked around the animal stalls for Solomon but could not find him anywhere. The animals were missing, too. I felt as empty as the ship. Lost. Tossed in the storm. This odd place was my home and now it was a shell. What had happened? Had the few people and animals already found work with one of the other circuses? I couldn't imagine never seeing any of them again. When I looked inside our stable home, all of Solomon's things were missing, even the Bible I read to him. I slumped down on my bed. Would I not even get to say good-bye to my friend? I would ask around until I found which circus had hired him.

Finally, I forced myself to roll up my own few possessions inside the holey wool blanket. I could not imagine working as a stable boy without the company of Solomon. I was happy to know that Zach was safe and with people who loved him, but I did not know whether I could accept the spinster sisters' offer. I had been on my own for months, earned my own keep. For the first time in my life I felt like I belonged somewhere, inside the walls of this circus.

This odd collection of people and animals had opened a door to me when nobody else would. This is the home I wanted, and it panicked me to think of being buckled into a proper world of rules and expectations once more. Like I was back at the orphanage somehow. I dropped to the floor again—what was I to do? I stood in the ruins of what my life had become.

"Do you know what this elephant will eat?" A voice startled me from behind. At first I didn't recognize him without his tall hat, but then I realized it was Lefty, a ticket man and grinder.

"She loves watermelon. Where's Mendeley?" I asked before thinking, and then knew the answer before he said it.

"Dead," he confirmed.

"The fever, then?" I asked, though I was certain of his answer.

"No. They say Tippo drowned him herself," Lefty answered, picking up a piece of hay and sticking it in the gap between his front teeth.

"I don't understand," I said.

"When old Tippo's cage busted during the storm, she plucked Mendeley out of his bed. They say she held him under the sea." I remembered Mendeley beating her about the trunk to get her in line before shows. Solomon's warning about never being cruel to an elephant echoed in my mind. Apparently elephants did hold grudges after all.

"Have mercy," I finally choked out from my shock. "Tippo drowned?"

"Went over with Mendeley." He picked at his teeth with a toothpick the whole time he spoke. Solomon hadn't told me what had happened to Tippo. Now I understood why. I jumped up from my bed and looked for Little Bet. She was outside my stall, but she didn't seem like herself. There was no movement to her at all. Relief filled me to see her, though I was sorry to learn of Tippo's fate. Little Bet seemed sad. Could elephants grieve? I didn't doubt it after learning about Tippo's revenge.

"Little Bet's going to follow them into the nether-world if I don't get her to take something soon." He sounded annoyed. Little Bet walked up to me then and made a deep rumbling sound. Did she recognize me? Her trunk touched the side of my face and then it dropped, hanging as useless as my arm once was.

"We can't let that happen!" I said, louder than I expected. Lefty's eyebrows rose in surprise at my out-burst.

"She's only got to last through tomorrow for me anyhow," he said, and slapped her behind the ear, rougher than I would've liked.

"What do you mean?" I asked, and pulled out a candy that I had in my pocket. I tried to tempt Little Bet with it. But her trunk had lost its curiousness and wouldn't even sniff the butterscotch. I stroked behind her ears like I knew she liked. I started searching through the barrels where we kept the nuts and other elephant treats.

"It's all gone. What ain't been stolen is gonna be sold off," Lefty said, and I caught a glimpse of a whiskey bottle sticking out of his back pocket.

I didn't know what to say. I led Little Bet over to the rainwater barrel. She stuck her trunk inside it and explored, but she would not drink.

"Everything that's left gets auctioned on Friday

morning." He kept talking though I wasn't paying much attention. I was trying to find anything that might tempt Little Bet. "Though no one is going to want this good-for-nothing rubber cow." He got my attention with that. A bull was the most valuable part of a show. Of course someone would want her.

"Why's that?" I asked, trying to sound like I wasn't all that interested. I knew he was the type that if you wanted something, the price went up.

"Ah, she eats more than she's worth. She don't know no tricks. She's the worst kind of hay burner."

"Is that why no one bought her yet?" I asked, because it seemed to me that most anything of value was long gone from this ghost of a ship.

"Yup. Lord Hathaway gave her to me days ago. Said I could keep whatever she brought."

"That was generous," I said, but I was thinking generous indeed for Lord Hathaway.

"I've spent all my money trying to tempt her appetite. It's all gone to waste," he said, but I wondered if it all had. He seemed well fed to me, and the bottle he had wasn't cheap either.

"She will usually eat most anything," I answered. "Little Bet's half goat." He didn't even smile at my joke.

"Well, I've bought her lamb and beef and she ain't touched none of it."

I didn't say it aloud, but I thought what a fool he was. Elephants never ate meat. I felt a little frog leap inside my chest. There was something I could do after all.

"Well, like I said, she need only last through the auction Friday. They'll probably kill her to make glue anyway," he said, kicking some tools out of his way and making a racket that echoed in the empty ship. "I don't much care either way."

"Well, I do. Let me go get her a watermelon. I passed a stand on my way here."

"Suit yourself," he answered.

I dropped my stuff and began running back off the ship—it felt good to have my legs running beneath me. It took just a few minutes to fetch the watermelon and bring it back and present it to Little Bet. Her eyes seemed to light up and she cracked open the dark green fruit with a single tap of her foot. Her trunk seemed to find life again and gently pulled out the pink flesh of the fruit and stuffed it into the triangle of her mouth.

"Do you know where Solomon is?" I asked Lefty, thinking he might be useful for at least this information.

"Which one was Solomon?" he asked, disinterested.

I hesitated for a moment to find words to describe

him and then answered, "The older Negro who knows something about near everything."

"Him. Oh, they sold him off yesterday, I think."

"What?" I asked. He could not be right about this, either. Not possible. "What . . ." I choked. "What do you mean?" My throat felt raw. This could not be. It could not. Solomon couldn't be sold off like a chair! Anger poured over me. Solomon was a person, and a free man besides!

"I heard tell he had some debts," Lefty said. "Hathaway sold him off to pay them."

"You lie," I yelled in Lefty's face. "Solomon had money." I pointed at him, remembering the leather pouch I'd seen Solomon stuff it into. "And his free papers, too. He's no slave!"

"He is now. Papers get destroyed," he said, and pushed me out of his face. I slumped to the floor. He had no reason to lie. Lefty shrugged his shoulders like it didn't matter at all. Like the papers that held Solomon's freedom were worth as much as a polishing rag.

"He's just a damn Negro anyway," he answered, and kicked a little dirt my direction. I didn't answer him. He would never understand.

"Look, kid, I need some supper. Sit here with Little Bet and I'll give you a dime," he answered, softening his tone suddenly. I thought he had burned through all his money.

"I can't stay," I answered. "I have to find out where Solomon went!"

"Lord," Lefty said, exasperated, rubbing his chin and spitting out the toothpick into the hay, "I told you. He's gone. Why, I bet he's picking cotton on some plantation already. Forget him."

"I can't forget him. He's . . . he's my friend."

"Sounds like you need to get yourself a new one," he answered with a snide voice.

"Where's Hathaway? I'm going to find out where Solomon went."

"Lord but you is stubborn! Hathaway is gone, too, long gone," he answered, and took off his cap and slapped it against his thigh. He was getting irritated with me, but I didn't care.

"How could he be gone, too? I thought you said he was going to auction off what's left."

"No. The bank is going to auction off what is left. Hathaway sold most everything of value and snuck off into the night."

"Wasn't this Hathaway's boat?" I was confused. I was still holding on to the image of Solomon in my head and I wasn't thinking clearly at all.

"You think he could pay for something like this out

of his own pocket? The bank owns this boat, boy. Ain't you a simpleton!" he said, his face showing the same irritation now that his voice held. But I didn't cotton to being called a fool.

"I'm no simpleton, I just never thought on it before."

"Well, it's the thoughts of rich men, I guess," he said, backing down from his fervor. "Men like you and me is just too busy trying to keep ourselves fed, ain't we?" He could make you angry and then sound like your friend, this man Lefty. I didn't like being with him, he confused me so. At least with Solomon I always knew exactly where I stood.

"Now, just watch that baby elephant for me for a spell while I go find something to eat." Lefty was irritating me now, so I let him go, if for nothing else, so I could think. I needed to sort through the stable and try to find any evidence of where Solomon may have gone.

Little Bet followed me into the stable and I tore it apart looking for any clue of Solomon. I even ripped open the straw mattresses and overturned the beds he had made. I checked under the base of the lantern for some secret message. There was none. Down into the straw I sank, overwhelmed with the knowledge that Solomon was gone. Sold back into his own nightmare of slavery.

I tried to hold back, but I cried for him until I was

dry. Little Bet stood beside me while I sobbed. She tried her old tricks to cheer me—her trunk tweaking my nose, rooting around my ear, and flipping my hair. She even pushed a piece of watermelon into my mouth, but its sudden sweetness choked me, so I spit it on the floor, unable to make my throat swallow it. She plucked it up for herself. Exhausted, I fell asleep on the remnants of my hay bed, Little Bet guarding my fitful dreams. It wasn't until first light that I realized Lefty had never returned.

CHAPTER

I WOKE UP to find Caleb standing over me and shaking my shoulders. Little Bet was like a massive shadow outside the stall, picking through the litter on the floor and silently stalking around in her freedom.

"I snuck out of the hotel to find you before Momma woke up!" He was nervous and he didn't often break the rules, I knew. He started gathering up my things and stuffing them into a pillowcase he'd brought from the hotel. It unnerved me to see him collecting my items, assuming I would go with him. When he lifted my old boots, a leather pouch fell out. It was Solomon's, and I snatched it off the dusty floor and squeezed it in my palm. He had left me a clue after all.

"Come on, now, Daddy is back from Pennsylvania,"

he said, and he kept stuffing my few clothes into the bag. "We'll be catching the train soon."

I started to follow Caleb. I needed to tell him about Zach and the spinsters' offer. When we walked out of my stable, there was Little Bet, searching through rubbish piled around the empty animal cages.

"I can't just leave Little Bet here."

"Ain't she being auctioned off with the boat?" Caleb asked.

"I don't think anyone will buy her," I answered, though a strange part of me was suddenly worried that someone might.

"Can you cage her with some food? Let the auctioneers deal with her tomorrow?"

"I can't just leave her behind."

"You've got to come speak to my pa about the stable job."

"About that. I, uh," I started to explain.

"Look, I've got to hurry back to the hotel. Let's meet outside the hotel restaurant in an hour," he said frantically, and then ran off with my stuff flung across his shoulder in the pillowcase. I didn't know what to do. I had to go see Mr. and Mrs. Greene and now Caleb had my things.

After Caleb left, I opened Solomon's pouch. Inside

were a couple of dollars in coins and a piece of paper that he'd been practicing writing his name on. It was scraggly and worn and it obviously took a great deal of effort to control his hand. On the back it said, "4 Oen," which must've been his attempt to spell my name. My throat closed with tears, but I forced myself to swallow them.

I tried to put Little Bet back in her original stall, but it was ruined. None of the others were near big enough to hold her. I had to take her with me to the hotel: I couldn't just leave her here. What if someone stole her?

I found a leather harness for Little Bet. We walked through the tattered remnants of the ring and out into the pink light of the morning. She was almost as large as the few carriages rumbling through the city. Her trunk's curiosity had recovered now, and I could've sworn that she was trying to talk to me with her low rumblings. It took me longer than I expected to reach the hotel since folks kept stopping me to pet her and ask about her. One man even handed me a quarter when Little Bet tipped the hat off his son's head and made him smile. He said the boy hadn't smiled since losing his mother to the yellow jack, and he was mighty grateful to see it again. Finally I made it to the fancy hotel.

Mr. and Mrs. Greene and Caleb waited for me in

the lobby. I guess I was easy to spot with Little Bet in tow because Caleb came right outside to meet me. Mr. Greene told Caleb to go back inside.

Mrs. Greene shook her head and asked, "What are you doing with that confounded nuisance, Owen?"

"Lefty never came back for her," I answered.

"No wonder, filthy beast." Mrs. Greene pinched her nose as Little Bet delivered a large pile of road apples behind her.

Mr. Greene spoke up finally, and his voice was firm. "You should take her back to the boat. It's her only chance to find a home."

"But he said no one will want her."

"Who would?" Mrs. Greene asked no one in particular.

"I would!" Caleb answered, coming out of the hotel.

"You should not be outside. Now get back in the hotel!" Mr. Greene said to Caleb, but not very sternly.

"I'm not going to get the yellow jack now," Caleb said.

"Do not tempt the fates," Mrs. Greene answered, and shooed him back inside. He stared out of a picture window while we continued talking.

"We're catching the train right after lunch, so we'll need to be rid of Little Bet by then," Mr. Greene said.

"I can't just abandon her!" I answered, surprised at

how much I meant it. But I realized that I didn't just mean Little Bet, I meant Solomon, too.

"Well, she can't ride on the train," said Mrs. Greene.

"I . . . I found my brother," I finally answered, though it wasn't the way I'd meant to tell them. I pulled out the crumpled telegram and handed it to Mrs. Greene.

"How lucky for you," Mrs. Greene said. Caleb's eyes widened behind the glass window, and he kept mouthing something though I couldn't tell what it was. I was trying to pay attention to Mr. Greene's advice about which train to take to Pennsylvania, but Caleb kept distracting me. Caleb must've been frustrated too because he burst out from behind the door, and Gwendolyn stood behind him smiling at me.

"What's happening?" Caleb asked.

"Owen found his brother," Mrs. Greene started to explain, "so he's going to go live with him in Pittsburgh."

"Oh," Caleb answered, clearly disappointed. "But I thought Owen might be like my own brother."

"Now, Caleb"—Mrs. Greene tousled his hair—"Owen has a brother who needs him. You know that."

"Pittsburgh won't be too far from us," Mr. Greene added. "We'll see Owen at least once a year."

"Ain't the same," Caleb answered, stuffing his hands in his pockets and kicking a pebble with his foot. "Ain't the same a'tall."

I didn't know what to say to Caleb to make him feel better. I felt sorry for him all of a sudden, not having a brother of his own. Despite his fine family and money, I guess he didn't have it perfect. Guess nobody did.

"Go on, now"—Mr. Greene patted Caleb's back—"and get Owen's things."

"Yes, sir," Caleb said.

While Caleb trotted off, Mr. Greene filled me in on the rest of train schedules and how to make the connections I'd need to get to Pittsburgh. He offered to have me ride with them, of course, but I told him I wanted to see to Little Bet first. He, at least, understood that. When Caleb came back with my stuff, it was in a fine brown leather case. Mrs. Green's eyebrows shot up when she saw it, but then she nodded at Caleb, giving him permission to let me have it, I guess.

Mr. Greene pressed ticket fare to Pittsburgh into my left hand and shook my right hand hard, like a man does. "Good luck to you, Owen." Gwendolyn gave me a paper bag with a couple of oatmeal-raisin cookies inside. And she kissed my cheek and squeezed my hand with her gloved one. Heat crawled up my neck and lit my ears afire.

Caleb hugged me in his stick arms for just a second, and Mrs. Greene patted me on the back and rested her hand on my shoulder for an extra moment. She smelled like my ma and I wondered whether I was making the right decision. Little Bet tried to touch Mrs. Greene's face with her trunk, but she shooed her away like a fly. The Greenes were a fine family, and I wouldn't have to be Quaker or nothing to be with them. When they walked back into their fancy hotel, I wondered if I'd ever see them again. I felt like someone was pressing his thumb into that soft space in my neck, but I hurt so much I had no tears left inside me. I turned away.

CHAPTER

I WALKED LITTLE BET back down toward the water to forage while I thought of a plan. Rationing out the food I had, I could make it last me for several days, as long as I could find places for her to forage. While I tossed ideas aside like empty nut shells, I practiced getting Little Bet to come to me when I called her by name. She would do it each time, as long as I shared a piece of cookie. No matter what others had said, she was not dumb or hard to train; she would do most anything for food. Of course, so would I.

Still, no solution presented itself to me. I had turned down a decent job and a home with the Greene family. Maybe they'd even come to think of me as their own son. And I'd have a horse of my own like Zach used to dream about. Of course, it would mean nothing without him to share it with. And then I got to thinking about Zach with the spinster sisters. Why hadn't they just adopted us when they'd had the chance? Of course it was because they had really wanted only Zach in the first place, not that I blamed them. Could I go live inside the tight walls of a Quaker world? Was it pity only that made them offer a bed to me? I was sure it was so. Still, I had to answer soon. I longed to see Zach, but I couldn't picture myself in their top-buttoned world anymore.

I thought of trying to auction poor Little Bet off. Lefty was right, though, no one would want her, leastways not yet. My head hurt and my neck was baking in the afternoon New Orleans sun. I needed water, and the lapping waves of salty water would not quench my sanded tongue.

We walked back up through the streets looking for a vendor or produce stand. Because of the fever many shops were closed and others stood vacant. But here and there a few folks were trying to sell what little they had. We walked toward the theater district. It, too, stood like a ghost town thanks to the fever. Even the large amphitheaters stood empty, everyone afraid of spreading the yellow jack.

Finally we found a stand offering summer fare. The old man's fruits and vegetables were loaded onto wooden shelves, tilted to tempt those riding by in a carriage or on horseback. The tomatoes were bright red and the corn a pale yellow. Squash, onions, watermelon, and cucumbers all looked delicious. I tried not to think of the various meals I'd had on the *Palace* with these vegetables, though my tongue seemed to remember by itself, and my mouth was suddenly so full of saliva that I had to swallow.

"Can I have a drink from your bucket?" I asked the old man. I got too close to his stack of tomatoes to ask because Little Bet grabbed four of them and tossed them, one after another, into her mouth. I was never going to get a sip now.

"What in hellfire!" the old man said, anger lighting up his eyes.

"Sorry, sir," I said, digging in my pocket for the change that would pay for them. When I offered it up, his face softened. Afraid that Little Bet would soon eat all my cash, I tied her to the horse-hitching post just out of reach of the ripe vegetables. He eyed me suspiciously but finally handed me the gourd to dip in the water. I drank three down and didn't mind that some splashed on my shirt to cool me off, either.

The old man started stacking up more watermelons onto the table that was closest to Little Bet. Her head began swaying back and forth, and I knew it was torture for her to see her favorite fruits. I had to get out of here, and fast. Before I could untie her, she pulled against the post and, without much effort, she snapped it like a twig. She bumbled over to the old man and startled him, tipping his hat onto the ground. When he bent to pick it up, she snagged another tomato and popped it into her mouth. He didn't see her do it!

"Seems like she wants one of these melons," the old man said.

"They're her favorites," I answered, trying not to laugh.

"Well, can she do any tricks? I might spare one if she could."

"None yet," I answered, getting an idea, "but I aim to teach her some."

Little Bet stood there with good manners and listened to us. She even looked from the old man to me like she was considering the offer. Suddenly she wrapped her trunk around the farmer and tipped his hat off his head. When he reached down to pick it up, she goosed him on the behind. I thought he might get mad again, but instead he laughed heartily.

"This one is a clown?" he asked. And I tried out a laugh too. He handed over the watermelon. "Move along then, before she eats everything I've grown." His face lightened, and I could tell this would be an encounter that would likely grow with each telling.

That night Little Bet and I camped on the beach. She played in the water with me and we splashed each other as the sun dropped into the water. She sucked up the water in her trunk and sprayed it above my head like a fountain, making pink diamonds in the fading light. Laughter bubbled out from a place I thought I had lost. I missed Solomon. I wondered where he might be at just this moment.

As I stared out to sea, Little Bet stayed nearby. She would wander off and forage for a bit, but she always came back after a short spell, like I was her momma. I unrolled my blanket onto the warm sand and stared up into the starry night. How could it have been only a week ago that Solomon and I talked under this blanket of stars? The one-eyed moon stared at me, uncaring, having witnessed it all. When I woke once in the middle of the night, Little Bet had stepped carefully over me, and her bulky gray body was now my tent and only home. Comforted, I fell back into sleep and into the storm of my dreams.

In them, Solomon was eating scrambled eggs at the carved table inside the spinster sisters' house. Caleb tamed lions and Mrs. Greene was dressed in a fancy clown's wardrobe. Lord Hathaway swam laps around the circus ring. Ostriches, panthers, and the lions sat as patrons in the fancy red upholstery of the *Palace's* best seats, waiting for the amusements to begin, snacking on their bags of nuts and sipping pink lemonade. Finally, the sun bursting over the water woke me, and I sat up under the pillars of Little Bet's legs. I knew what I had to do.

CHAPTER

I LED LITTLE BET back toward the *River Palace*. When we arrived, there was already a crowd beginning to form for the auction. It was more people than I expected, considering the recent epidemic. Apparently greed and a bargain made many risk their health. That or they were survivors and no longer afraid of it. Little Bet seemed to know something was wrong. She did not try to leave me and only picked at the grass and weeds while I spoke briefly to the auctioneer about terms. Everything about him was drab—his hair, beard, suit, and even his shoes. I did not know if his terms were fair, but I had no other options so I took them. Little Bet and I found some shade under a giant live oak tree and waited for the bidding to begin. She pulled at the air plant that hung like ragged hair from the tree and began tossing it around to amuse herself.

Fancy chairs that had been spared damage were sold so cheap, I could've bought them with the coins in my pocket. Odd things from the ship like stray tools and canned food and the printing press I had worked with for so many weeks sold for very little. Even items that could be of use only to another circus went—like cages, costumes, and props.

I was not prepared for the next thing up for auction.

"People will see double with this next offering!" the auctioneer guffawed as suddenly, on stage, were Molly-Catherine, the twins.

Molly-Catherine stood, hands clasped together in the front. Pride and anger were etched across the sisters' youthful faces. Both stared off into the clouds as if to avoid the terrible display before them. I felt as though Little Bet were sitting on my chest and I could not breathe. I thought Molly-Catherine were free people, just like Solomon. They had fancy clothes! I assumed they had bought their freedom like he had, but here they were being sold like livestock.

"Prepare to make thousands of dollars displaying the lovely two-headed nightingale. Sing something for us, darlin'."

The girls began one of their favorite songs, one I had

heard them sing many times, and the sweet sound of their voices hushed the immense crowd before them.

Over the billows away and away;
Ours is the freedom that knows no decay.
Braving the tempest, and stemming the tide,
In safety forever we glide, we glide.

"We'll start the bidding at twenty thousand," the auctioneer said.

The crowd gasped. A slave generally cost around a thousand, give or take. I studied the people bidding on their lives. I wondered whether they would find a kind or a cruel master. Would they be displayed in a cage, naked as the day they were born, like Solomon had said they were long ago? It made me ill to consider. As much as I had hated Hathaway, I realized that until now he had taken good care of these two, at least.

When it was all said and done, the twins were bought for thirty thousand dollars. Anger lit through me from my feet to the tips of my ears. Had Solomon been sold on a block like this or was he passed between greedy hands in the cloak of night? I was determined to hear the story from his own lips.

My stomach felt suddenly sour and I retched, nearly on my own boots. I lifted up a silent prayer for the twins' safety. I did not want to stay, but I had no other options. Though I did not cotton to making this auctioneer any richer, he called to me as I wiped my mouth on the tail of my shirt. I had made a deal and shook the man's hand. Our deal, like it or not, was done.

"And here we have a fine young elephant," he said to the crowd, pointing over at Little Bet and me. Standing up straight, I hoped to show the same grace and courage that Molly-Catherine had, though it wasn't my freedom to be sold. I swallowed back tears, thinking of selling my new friend to the highest bidder before me.

"This fine pachyderm has just now reached the age to begin training," the auctioneer said confidently, so sure sounding that I practically believed the lie myself. "An elephant needs time to learn our language." It made sense; perhaps it was even true.

At first no one made a bid. I was afraid that I might get stuck with the care of Little Bet, and I didn't know how to provide for myself, let alone her. Whispers crossed through the crowd, but still no one made a bid.

"She could be sold to a Northern factory," the auctioneer announced, "for glue, at a fine profit."

The bidding began. It was slow. I did not know if I could bear the knowledge that my friend could be turned to glue. My knees shook. Perhaps I could just leave the auction and take my chances with her. No. I needed the money to help find and free Solomon. I hated myself at that moment, but I planted my feet in the earth. I could not look at Little Bet.

"Five dollars!" yelled a man from the back.

"Ten," said another, without much enthusiasm.

"Twenty-five dollars," proclaimed a woman in the front dressed in a wide tiered gown. I had heard tell that some rich folks kept odd animals for their own amusement. Was she one of these? I prayed it was so and that she would win the bidding.

"Fifty!" said a bearded man in the front row. The bidding ceased.

"Sold!" said the auctioneer. It wasn't much for a pachyderm. If Little Bet had been trained, I bet she'd have gone for thousands.

The bearded man came up to us after all the other items were sold, including the shell of the *River Palace* herself.

I handed him the leather lead and dropped my head, for I did not want him to see the tears that betrayed me. He handed me twenty-five dollars, half of what she had brought. The auctioneer took the other half. Instead of feeling excited, I felt as though I'd been kicked in the stomach.

"What's your name?" the man asked me.

"Owen Burke, sir," I answered, though I didn't understand why he bothered with my name.

"How much for you?" the man asked me.

"I am not for sale!" I answered. I had seen enough flesh sold today. No one would count me as property.

"I mean for your salary," he said with a wide smile, his blue eyes dancing.

"Salary?" I asked, confused.

"You don't work for free, I imagine," he answered.

"Of course not," I answered. I looked up to study the man who was offering me a salary. I had not recognized him at first, but now that I saw him square on, I realized he was none other than Dan Rice, the most famous clown in all America. His likeness had been on posters everywhere and in newspapers across the country. He wore an outfit when he performed that looked like the flag itself. Everyone knew Dan Rice had the finest circus with the best animals. I was surprised he wanted Little Bet at all.

"Thirty a month plus room and board," he offered, "but you'll work twelve-hour days, six days a week, to get her ready for my new show."

I did the math in my head quickly. With what I had saved, plus Solomon's money and Little Bet's money, it would take me years. Still, I had to try.

"Well, son, I don't have all day," he said, crossing his arms over his skinny chest.

"Make it forty, Mr. Rice," I offered boldly, "and you've got yourself a deal."

"All right, then," he answered, smiling, and his eyes seemed to dance inside his pointed face. His white hair and goatee were striking, and I could see how he kept audiences spellbound. There was something about him that made you want to stay nearby.

"My plan is for her to travel on my new showboat, not perform at the amphitheater. Is that a problem for you?" he asked. I had heard Dan Rice was going to start a circus boat, too—one that would compete with the *Palace*. I guess he didn't have to worry about the *Palace* anymore.

"Will it travel up to Pittsburgh?" I asked.

"Yes, of course, all of the river towns. We only play New Orleans in winter."

"Yes! Yes!" I was thrilled. This way I'd be able to see Zach at least once a year! My heart somersaulted inside my chest.

"I can also help out in the press room." I thought quickly, trying to figure out how to earn even more money. "I can set type and even write advertisements."

"Well, you are a find, Owen Burke." Relief swept over me as I realized that Little Bet would not be glue and that I would take care of her myself.

I offered my hand to seal the agreement. He shook my hand hard but looked me square in the eyes with an intense stare. His eyes were lit like there was a candle behind them. Then a smile swept across his face. I could tell he was a man you could trust. It would be a welcome change to work with someone so forthright. I had to ask him one thing though. "But can I ask a question?"

"Of course." He smiled down at me. Dan Rice was one tall fellow.

"Why would you take a chance on Little Bet?" I asked.

He clapped me on the back and we started walking toward the street. "As Voltaire once said, 'His Sacred Majesty, Chance, decides everything.'"

I tried not to look as confused as I felt with his answer, but my face betrayed me.

Mr. Rice laughed. "What are we if not the chances we take?"

That I understood. "I appreciate the chance you're offering me, sir."

"We'll get started this afternoon," he answered, dropping the leather lead. "Meet me back at the amphitheater in an hour. I assume you know where it is."

"Of course. Everyone knows your theater, sir." Then he tipped his tall hat and walked through the crowd. My knees fairly wobbled with the last half hour and so

I plunked down under a live oak tree to get my wits about me. Little Bet foraged around the trash the crowd left behind while I let myself think. It was a fair offer Mr. Rice had made, especially for someone so young; I was glad I'd taken it without hesitation. But somehow I wished I could still get to Pittsburgh and tell Zach all about my summer so he might understand my choice. First Momma left him behind, and now me. But I owed Solomon, and I knew Zach was better off with the spinsters. I realized, as I had not allowed myself to before, that Momma also had suffered with her decision to leave us at the orphanage. Though I had made such a habit of pushing Momma out of my mind, I let myself picture her face torn by despair and determination standing on the orphanage steps. Understanding, though not quite forgiveness, wrapped itself around me.

Little Bet and I had only one more thing left to do. At the telegraph office I sent a cable to the spinster sisters and Zach. It pleased me to know that those two women were doting on Zach. I consoled myself knowing that he would get all the book learning he loved and maybe even get to college! I owed them the world.

Happy Zach's home STOP My home's in the circus STOP Long letter follows STOP

{ 193 }

Little Bet and I walked toward the theater district. She threw her trunk over my shoulder and explored my ear with its wet tip, making me laugh aloud. I couldn't wait to start trying to train her with Dan Rice this afternoon. Tonight, when I could steal some time away from Little Bet, I would tell Zach this story from the beginning. Maybe I should've listened to him the day I climbed the elm, I'd tell him, but despite it all, I was glad I hadn't. I took a chance the day I jumped off the train and now I understood why. And I had one task, one goal now. This oath was mine: I would find my friend Solomon and I would see him free.

AUTHOR'S NOTE

The *River Palace* is based on the historical ship the *Floating Palace*, which was owned and operated by Rogers and Spalding in the 1850s. While historians provided intriguing facts about this circus era, I have taken liberties with the details for my story.

America was moving from an agricultural nation to an industrial one, but back-breaking labor six days a week was the norm for most of the population during the 1850s. When the circus came to town (by wagon, rail, or ship), it was often deemed a public holiday for adults and children alike. Circus history is filled with vibrant anecdotes, compelling characters, and fascinating details—and I have been honored to spend the past year inside their world.

There were many showboats during this golden age of river travel, many of them falling under the wide umbrella of circus entertainment. Often they used the rivers as a form of easy transportation between towns and pitched a traditional circus tent when they arrived. The *Floating Palace* was so unique because the two thousand or more ticket holders boarded the ship and watched the show on board and in great luxury for the time period.

The Fugitive Slave Act of 1850 made it a crime to harbor the escape of any slave, even in a free state. People faced six months in prison and a hefty fine if they aided an escaped slave. A captured person had no rights to a trial by jury, or to even testify on their own behalf. This law fanned the flames that led to the Civil War because it forced Northerners to become complicit in an institution many of them despised. Despite the risks, many people bravely helped slaves escape to the safety of Canada. Though it was rare for a free man (or woman) to be sold back into slavery, it did, on occasion, happen. Court battles that started by tracing the sale of these people occasionally led to their freedom.

Yellow fever hit New Orleans in 1853 and wiped out over six thousand residents in a single summer. Mosquitoes weren't discovered as the hosts until much later, and the disease was controlled with a vaccine. It devastated many cities over hundreds of years and was fearfully avoided. The storm on the gulf coast was also a real event and the *Floating Palace* did have to be cut from its tow to avoid shipwreck.

The conjoined twins, Molly-Catherine, were inspired by the real-life twins Millie-Christine. Other people exhibited on the ship for their birth defects were all real individuals who worked in circuses of that time period. The real Millie-Christine were born slaves, kidnapped, and put on performance circuits, and subject to every degradation imaginable. When slavery ended, Millie-Christine became quite wealthy, finally able to earn a profit off their own display. They became great philanthropists, offering many scholarships to former slaves.

Other human oddities like the armless man, bearded woman, and skeleton man were common on the circus bills of the period. Eventually, of course, it became unpopular to display people born with differences and to profit off them. To modern readers it seems particularly cruel, but at the time, it may have saved many of these folks from lives in abysmal institutions where people with disabilities were often kept in cages and leg irons. In the circus, at least, they created families for themselves and had the opportunity to earn a living.

Dan Rice was the most famous American entertainer in the 1800s. His distinctive looks and costume were the inspiration for the "Uncle Sam" figure

Americans know today. He gave astounding clown performances (which were more like stand-up comedy and theater than the antics associated with clowns today). He operated a circus ship and had a grand amphitheater in New Orleans, though he lost his fortune several times over the course of his career.

If you'd like to learn more about circus history, I highly recommend a visit to the Circus World Museum in Baraboo, Wisconsin. They have wonderful exhibits and an archive so Amazing! Spectacular! Mammoth! you won't believe your eyes!

ACKNOWLEDGMENTS

I gratefully acknowledge my family and friends who sustained me while writing this novel. First, to Randy Zimmer for support, both literal and figurative. Much love to Cole and Abbie for eating squiggly noodles just one.more.time. Thanks also to Trish DeLong, Pauline and Werner Schwitalski, Jeff and Susan Greene, Jane Fischer, Jackie Bowker, Jessica Swaim, Kyra Teis, the STAKS, the SCLB, Linda Sue Park and the PUB, and my amazing agent, Barry Goldblatt, for their insightful comments and cheerleading. I'm greatly indebted to Erin Foley and the whole Circus World Museum for access to their immense library and original sources. Errors are completely my own. Melanie Cecka, thanks for taking a chance on a few chapters and big ideas, and thanks to the entire Bloomsbury staff for their wondrous creativity and passion. Without Julia Durango this novel would not exist.